"A brilliant success . . . more beautifully conceived and executed than anything I have read in a long time. . . . Charles Webb is an important writer."

—*Washington Post*

"Hilarious, breakneck-paced, loaded with surprises . . . the same blend of matter-of-fact absurdity, refreshing irreverence and startling insights which made THE GRADUATE *such a delight."*

—*Philadelphia Bulletin*

"Subtle and artful . . . exposes the malaise of love and marriage today."

—*Los Angeles Times*

"There are a lot of laughs in this book, and most of them are nervous; if there is much that is funny, there is damned little that is droll. The scene in the dirty movie theatre is nothing short of wonderful."

—*Book World*

The Marriage of a Young Stockbroker

by Charles Webb

A SIGNET BOOK from
NEW AMERICAN LIBRARY
TIMES MIRROR

Library of Congress Catalog Card Number 79-103601

This is an authorized reprint of a hardcover edition published by J. B. Lippincott Company.

SIGNET TRADEMARK REG. U.S. PAT. OFF. AND FOREIGN COUNTRIES
REGISTERED TRADEMARK—MARCA REGISTRADA
HECHO EN CHICAGO, U.S.A.

SIGNET, SIGNET CLASSICS, SIGNETTE, MENTOR and PLUME BOOKS
are published by The New American Library, Inc.,
1301 Avenue of the Americas, New York, New York 10019

FIRST PRINTING, AUGUST, 1971

PRINTED IN THE UNITED STATES OF AMERICA

The Marriage of a Young Stockbroker

Part One

ONE

After the shower William dried himself off, put on his clothes and walked down the hall to the entrance of the kitchen. Lisa was fixing dinner. He watched her empty a package of frozen peas into a pan, then turn on the burner. "Lisa?" he said. "Are you bored here at the beach?"

She glanced at him.

"Are you?"

"No." She walked to the icebox.

"I mean what did you expect down here," he said. "Could I ask you that."

"Nothing." She opened the door of the icebox and removed another package of frozen food.

William turned around and walked slowly across the cork floor into the living room. He seated himself on a chair beside the large bay window. He looked for several minutes down at the beach below. Then he got up and returned to the door of the kitchen. "Lisa, please tell me what's on your mind." He watched her lift two plates down from a cupboard.

"Do you want to eat outside?" she said. "Or in the dining alcove."

"The alcove."

She set the plates on a shelf, then opened a drawer and removed several pieces of silverware.

"Lisa," he said, stepping into the kitchen, "we have twelve more days down here."

She lifted two napkins out of the drawer.

"Lisa?"

"I know we have twelve more days."

"But if they're going to be like this one and yesterday, why don't we just go back home and I'll go back to work. Work is fun compared to this."

"Excuse me." She carried the silverware and napkins past him and into the dining alcove.

William walked to the icebox, opened it and removed two cans of beer. "Maybe we haven't adjusted to being on vacation yet," he said, carrying the cans into the other room. He handed one to his wife.

She opened it and took a sip, then walked back into the kitchen.

"Lisa?"

"I'm getting dinner."

"But could we just sit here for a few minutes?"

She returned and seated herself. William sat down on the chair across from hers and rested his feet on a stool. "How about this beach," he said, "does it seem like a good one?"

"Yes."

"It seems all right to me." He took a sip from the can and turned to look out the window. "I'd say we were quite lucky."

His wife was looking out at the ocean.

"Wouldn't you say we were quite lucky on this house, Lisa?"

"Yes."

"Would you?" he said. "Or is there something about it you don't like."

"I like it."

He looked out the window again. They sat quietly for several moments, then Lisa glanced down at her wristwatch.

"What shall we do after dinner," William said.

"I don't know," she said. "I guess what we did last night."

"Did you find that a satisfying evening?"

"Yes."

"To sit there three hours reading the *Reader's Digest* condensation of Captain Hornblower while I read magazines seemed satisfying."

She took a sip of her beer.

"Did it?"

"It was relaxing," she said. "I don't understand what you expect down here."

William moved forward on his chair and held out one of his hands. "Think of something you want to do, Lisa."

She ran her finger around the top of the beer can. "What do *you* want to do."

"Lisa."

"Why should *I* think up the thing to do."

"Because if you thought it up, you'd want to do it. If I thought it up you might not."

She took a sip of her beer. "You can't think of anything then."

"I can," he said. "I saw a movie down the coast. I can't remember its name but it seemed like a good one."

"Let's go to it."

"But Lisa," he said, pointing at her, "I want you to have an idea."

She looked down at a square of cork tile flooring beside the leg of her chair. "You don't want me to read."

"Do you *want* to read again?" He reached out and rested his hand on her knee. "Lisa," he said, "we're here at the beach; here in our rented house."

"I know."

"We planned for it, saved up for it. We did all that, didn't we."

"Yes."

"And now we're here; we've come."

She nodded.

"We've packed all the things we'll need for two weeks, put them in the car. . . ."

"Bill."

He reached down and tapped his forefinger on one of the cork tiles. "I'm just trying to bring it home," he said, hitting the tile with his whole hand, "that here we are at the beach!"

She looked back at him without saying anything, then glanced toward the kitchen.

Finally William leaned back in his chair and looked out the window again at a breaking wave. It foamed up over the sand, then the white froth sank down and disappeared. A broken wooden box had been washed up onto the beach. William let his eyes rest on it a few moments. He was about to turn back toward his wife and speak again when something else caught his eye.

Suddenly he moved forward on his chair and set his feet on the floor. "What's that," he said, pointing out to sea.

"Where."

"Right there." He got up from his chair. "On the other side of the buoy."

Lisa moved her head closer to the glass and squinted.

"See it?"

"Where."

"I'll get the binoculars." William hurried over to a bookcase in the corner and removed a black leather case. He opened it quickly as he walked back toward the window, then reached inside and pulled out a pair of binoculars. Standing in front of the window he raised the instrument to his eyes. He turned one of the eyepieces, then the other. "It's a whale," he said. He adjusted the eyepiece again. "Here." He removed the beer can from his wife's hand and gave her the binoculars. "Half way between the buoy and the rocks." She raised them to her eyes. "Almost to the rocks now," he said.

"I don't see it."

William got down on his knee, took the glasses from her and found the moving black shape again. "I'll hold them." She bent her head down and looked through them. "Sort of undulating along," he said.

"Wait."

"See it?"

"That's the buoy."

"It's disappearing." William stood, put the binoculars to his eyes again and watched as the large whale moved out to the rocks, then swam around them. He continued holding the binoculars up to his eyes several moments after the animal had gone out of sight, then lowered them again. "You didn't see it."

"No."

He looked down at her for a few moments, then picked up the case and fitted the binoculars into it. He sat down and picked up his beer can.

They sat quietly, looking out at the orange sun resting on the horizon; then finally Lisa got up from her chair.

"Where are you going."

"To get dinner."

"Let's finish our drinks first."

Lisa looked down at her beer can, then seated herself across from her husband again.

The next time the binoculars were put into use was the following evening. William was in the same chair, his feet propped up on the stool. A magazine was resting on his lap but he hadn't looked at it for half an hour. Instead he was looking at the large window beside him and at the reflection of his wife.

In a corner of the room, under a lamp, Lisa Alren sat reading a book. William watched her turn a page. Her eyes moved downward, she reached up to move a few strands of hair back behind one of her ears, then she lowered her hand and turned another page.

A wave rolled in, its foam illuminated by a spotlight from another house on the cliff. When the foam had sunk into the sand, William looked up again at the reflection of his wife. She raised her hand up over her mouth to cover a cough. Then William noticed another light.

He looked at it a moment, then moved his head forward to see it better. It was a fire at the other end of the beach, the figures of several girls standing around it in bathing suits. He glanced again at Lisa, then picked the magazine up off his lap and rested it on the floor. He set his feet down.

Lisa turned her head. "Did you see something?"

"Just waves."

She looked back at her book.

William got up and walked slowly across the room to the bookcase. He stood in front of it a few moments studying the backs of some books, then reached out very slowly for the binoculars. He unfastened the clasp at the top of the case, then reached inside and slowly lifted up the black instrument. He moved it around against his side, away from his wife.

Lisa turned her head around to look at him.

"I'm looking for a book."

She looked at his face for a moment, then turned back to the book.

"Here's one." He removed a book from the shelf. "Maybe I'll take it in the bathroom." Carrying the binoculars at his side he walked past his wife and in through the door of the bathroom. He closed, then locked it. He lowered the seat of a toilet just inside the door, banged on it, then walked quickly to the window. He set his book down, then pulled a thin curtain back from in front of the glass. By moving his head to the edge of the window he could see past the next house and down onto the beach, where there was an orange glow from the bonfire. He moved his head back and raised the binoculars up to his eyes. He twisted one eyepiece, then moved them up against the glass of the window. Down next to the bonfire, seated on a log in the sand, were two girls in bathing suits, the light from the fire shining up against their legs and arms.

William lowered the binoculars. He glanced back at the door of the bathroom, then turned around again and very slowly unfastened the lock in the center of the window, clearing his throat loudly as he did. With both hands he opened the window as wide as it would go. Outside was a small concrete patio. A clothesline ran from the wall of the house to a fence. William fixed the strap of the binoculars over his shoulder, then slowly put one leg out the window and stepped onto the patio. He moved forward and brought his other leg out after him. When he was all the way out he turned around and slowly closed the window.

In front of the house was a small grass yard and at its far edge, separating it from the sea cliff, a law wall. Looking up at the lighted window above, William moved quickly along beside the wall, crouching over so the light from the living room wouldn't fall on him. He stopped at the center of the wall, then holding the binoculars against his hip, quickly stood up on his tiptoes for an instant and looked into the room at his wife, still reading in her chair in the corner. He crouched down again, turned and held the binoculars up to his eyes, quickly aiming them toward the bonfire. Two other girls, one of them in a white T-shirt and one in a bathing suit, were standing on the other side of the fire. Another, eating a hot dog, was seated cross-legged in the sand. William looped the binocular strap around his neck, ducked down and ran to the top of the stairs. He seated himself and hurriedly removed his shoes and socks. Then he walked down the concrete steps and jumped into the cool sand.

The spotlight was in front of the house beside William's and shone down across a large area of the beach. But by staying very close to the cliff William was able to make his way down toward the other end of the beach without moving into the lighted area. As he moved quietly along the dark base of the cliff he bumped into a wooden rowboat, then slowly felt his way along it and to the other side. He stopped once to look back up toward his house but was unable to see it past an outcropping of cliff.

Beyond the rowboat were some steps leading up to a house. Then there was an open space of sand. Keeping his head down, William hurried across it and moved up against the cliff again. He waited a moment, then moved slowly out toward a large rock rising up from the sand. When he reached it he got down onto his knees, then moved forward till he could see around its edge.

Several more girls were around the bonfire that he hadn't seen before, and on the other side a man in an apron was holding a box of hot-dog rolls and passing them out. William got down onto his stomach at the edge of the rock and raised the binoculars up in front of his face. He turned the knob on the left eyepiece and focused on a girl twisting a hot dog onto a piece of wire. When it was on she walked up to the fire, crouched down and dangled it over some coals. William studied the top part of her bathing suit, the line between her breasts, then moved the binoculars slowly to the right. Another girl was turned part way around doing something to the side of her bathing suit. William inched forward on his elbows. He watched as she pulled off a button, looked at it a moment, then held it out to show one of the other girls.

Closer to the bonfire another rock was jutting up out of the sand. But to get to it he would have to pass across a space of sand illuminated by the spotlight. William looked back up over his shoulder toward the light, then at the other rock again. Finally, staying on his stomach, he began moving forward through the sand.

When he got just to the edge of the lighted space he stopped, glanced over toward the bonfire for a moment, then began moving quickly along the sand again, keeping his face down close to the ground.

"Hey," a girl said, "who's that."

He stopped. He was directly in the center of the lighted area.

"It's someone with binoculars."

William turned his face the other way, then quickly got to his feet. Keeping his face turned, he hurried back to his first rock.

"Mr. Van Meter?" a girl said. "Somebody was sneaking up on us."

"Where."

William glanced quickly up at the slant of the cliff several yards away.

"He went over by that rock."

Looping the binocular strap over his neck and turning the binoculars so they fell down against his back, William leapt up against the cliff. He clambered up, grabbing at a bush, then pulled himself up onto a flat space just as the bush pulled free from the soil, pebbles falling down onto the beach.

"Hello?" the man said.

William crawled quickly over some cold plants that squashed under his knees. At one place he began slipping down off the cliff but grabbed another bush and kept himself from falling.

"He was right over here," a girl said below him.

Immediately ahead was the broad beam of light shining down from the spotlight above. William stopped when he got to the edge of it, got to his feet, took the binoculars in his hand, then ran forward, keeping one hand over his face and trying to keep his balance on the slippery plants and slanted cliff.

"Up there! Look!"

"Stop!"

William fell, then scrambled to his feet without removing his hand from his face. He hurried on across and into the darkness at the other side of the light. Then he sat down. He was breathing heavily. He gulped in several mouthfuls of air and looked back down where he had been. Out from his rock, standing in the light, a girl was looking upward, shielding her eyes with one of her hands. "It was like a shadow going right past there," she said, pointing.

Mr. Van Meter stepped out from behind the rock into the light and looked up, also shielding his eyes with his hand. Then several other girls stepped up and looked up. William got to his feet quickly and began moving on along the cliff again.

"There!" a girl said. "In the dark!"

He ran faster, crouching closer to the ground.

"See him?"

"You!"

William began slipping again, grabbed a bush and pulled himself onward.

"Stop!"

Several yards ahead was the low wall separating his beach house from the top of the cliff. He reached it and threw himself over and onto the grass on the other side, landing on his side on the binoculars. He groaned, then turned over and held his ribs where the instrument had been crushed against him. He raised his head up to the level of the top of the wall and looked over with one eye. The man and several girls were still standing where they had been before, looking up. They were talking, but too far away for William to hear anything. He lowered his head. After massaging his side for a few moments, he crawled along the wall to where his shoes and socks were. When they were on he tiptoed toward the house. A leaf crackled as he stepped on it. He waited, then moved along beside the house and opened the window of the bathroom. He lifted his leg and put it over the sill, then moved forward and brought his other leg in after him. Then he turned around and closed the window. He drew the curtain back over the glass and reached down for the book, then walked over to the toilet and sat down. He pulled up the side of his shirt and looked at the bruise on his ribs—it was red. He removed the binoculars from his neck and put them up under his arm, under his shirt, then put the shirt down again and reached over for the toilet paper. He pulled some out, tore it off and crumpled it. He dropped it down into the toilet between his legs, then did it with another piece. Finally he cleared his throat and stood. He turned around and flushed the toilet. As it was flushing he dropped its lid, letting it bang loudly, and unlocked the door.

Lisa was still sitting in the corner, the book on her lap. She glanced up as her husband entered the room. He nodded at her.

"Did you find a good book?" she said.

"So-so; it's a little slow to start." He walked past her and to the bookcase again, removed the binoculars and slipped them back into their case. Then he closed the top of the case and stepped back from the book shelves. "Actually, it's dull." He looked down at his book's cover. "I may not go on with it." He returned it to the opening in the top shelf where it had been before, then stretched his arms out and yawned.

"Sleepy?" Lisa said.

"It's the sea air," he said, "do you mind if I turn in?"

"Go ahead."

"Good night," he said, starting up the stairs. His wife turned another page.

They ate lunch the next day about one o'clock. When they were done William broke a stem of green grapes from a bunch in a bowl. He carried it into the living room to the window and looked down at people on the sand.

After rinsing their dishes and setting them in the sink Lisa came out of the kitchen, walked past him to the foot of the stairs. "I'll be leaving between two and three," she said.

William turned around to look at her. "Where are you going."

"Before lunch you said we might have an outing this afternoon," she said. "Do you remember?"

"Yes."

She walked over to him and looked down at his wristwatch. "It's just after one," she said. "As long as we're back here by three I could go with you."

William looked at his watch, then at his wife. "Do you have an errand?"

She walked back to the other side of the room. "No," she said, "I'm leaving."

"Leaving for what."

"I'm leaving you, William."

He looked across the room at her a few moments.

"Do you understand now."

He didn't answer.

"I'm going to take a vacation, William," she said, "from you."

William rested the grapes on a table beside him.

It was quiet for a moment, except for a wave breaking on the sand below, then Lisa walked over to the chair beside a telephone table and seated herself. "I'm going up to stay with Nan and Chester for a while," she said.

"No, Lisa."

"Yes."

"I'm sorry," he said. "No."

"I called the cab company this morning while you were down on the beach. There'll be a taxi for me here around three."

He looked down at his grapes, then back across the room to the chair with his wife in it. "Did you tell them you wanted a ride to San Marino—seventy miles?"

"Yes."

William pointed at the phone. "Call them back."

She shook her head.

"Tell them you've changed your mind."

"But I haven't." She looked up at him. "Don't

worry though, you won't have to pay the cab fare."

"Right now. Call."

Lisa got up and walked into the kitchen, then returned, putting on her wristwatch.

"Who *is* going to pay for your fare."

"Nan."

"Did you talk to her too?"

"I didn't have to," she said, seating herself again. "Nan's told me she'd pay the fare if I took a taxi from the East Coast to San Marino." She held the watch up to her ear. "She's told me that many times: 'If he ever gets too much for you, get in a taxi and come to me. It doesn't matter where you are.' "

William lowered himself onto the couch. "If I get too much for you."

"You finally have."

"Could I ask how?"

"You know how, Bill," she said. "Last night. I don't want to talk about it."

He looked out at the ocean. A small girl was trying to stand up on a rubber raft, sunlight sparkling and glittering against the moving water around her.

"You're having your vacation," she said. "Now I'm going to take mine."

He looked back at her. "I'm sorry about last night, Lisa. I was going to tell you. I apologize for doing such a stupid thing."

She shook her head.

"I've been reprimanding myself all morning for doing it."

"I don't want to talk about last night," she said. "That's not the reason. I don't know the reason. Or if I do I can't say it."

"Could you try?"

She got up from her chair and walked slowly to the window. "I wouldn't succeed."

"Could you try though."

She stood looking down at people in their bathing suits on the sand.

"Or is it presumptuous of me to ask you to try."

"No," she said, "it's just that I've already tried. Over the past year, either by saying something to you or by not saying anything, I've tried. And I can't."

"You want a vacation from me."

"Yes."

"And it's not what happened last night."

"No."

"Is it the sight of me?" he said, putting his fingers against his chest. "Are you tired of looking at me?"

"I don't know," she said. "Yes."

William looked down at his knee. "What am I supposed to do about that."

"Nothing."

"Go around in a Halloween mask?"

"I'm just leaving," she said, facing him. "There's no way to explain it. If there was I wouldn't have to go."

William got up. "You're leaving because you're tired of me visually?"

"Yes—but I wouldn't be if I wasn't tired of you first in other ways."

"What ways."

"I don't know," she said, "your mannerisms . . ."

"Which mannerisms."

"All of them."

"Name one mannerism you're tired of."

"I don't know," she said, "flicking your ear . . ."

"Like this?"

She watched as he flicked his ear.

"You're tired of my doing that."

"Yes."

"Do I do it much?"

"Yesterday you stood here in the middle of the living room for fifteen minutes doing it."

"I didn't."

"I don't want to argue."

"Lisa," he said, walking over beside her, "let's assume I flicked my ear for fifteen minutes yesterday. I thank you for telling me; it must have been subconscious.

However, now that I know about it, now I know it's annoying, I promise I won't do it again."

She continued looking down at the beach.

"Okay, Lisa?" He reached for her arm. "I'll stop all my mannerisms if you want."

"How."

"I'll find a way," he said. "Sit down." He started leading her across the room but she stopped and withdrew her hand.

"Lisa . . ."

"It's your attitude toward me that I don't like," she said, turning to face him, "and I've never liked it."

William gestured toward a chair.

"When you're at work I don't have to live with it all day. On the weekends I can endure it. Before we were married it didn't seem so bad. But now, the thought of it for two weeks, day and night, is more than I want to think about. If you have to know, that's why I'm going to stay with Nan and Chester: your attitude toward me."

William picked up one of the chairs by the bay window and carried it to the center of the room to place behind his wife. "Try sitting down."

"No, Bill."

"Really," he said, "because I think we can solve this. My attitude toward you. It seems like we're getting down to the roots of the problem."

Lisa walked back to the window. "I'm not trying to be drastic," she said. "I'm not thinking of a divorce or anything like that. I'm just asking for the privilege of having my vacations away from you."

"My attitude," William said. "Could you be more specific?"

"No."

"The way I act toward you?" he said. "Is that . . .?"

"Yes."

"The way I act."

"William," she said, turning around to face him, "you can't grasp the problem because it's everything. It's just the way you are, the way we are together."

"Would you say I'm not fun to be with? Would that express it?"

Lisa nodded. "That's as close as I could come to expressing it." She walked past him and into the kitchen.

William followed.

Lisa took a glass down from the cupboard, turned on the faucet and filled it. "I feel pestered, harassed, pried at. All the time." She took a drink of water.

"Could I say one thing."

"You may say what you would like." She finished the water.

"Not to be abrupt," he said, "but what about yourself, your own attitude."

"That's my problem."

"I'm wondering if you think it's fun to be with a person who reads all the time on the vacation. A person who doesn't speak ninety-nine percent of the time. Who never jokes."

She set down the glass and turned. "You see . . ."

"Really."

"This is what I'm talking about." She pointed at him. "All the time. 'Why don't I have ideas, why don't I talk more, why don't I tell jokes.' What right do you have telling me to tell jokes."

"Not even joke though," he said, "maybe just smile. One smile a day."

"I'll smile," she said, looking out the window. "Just wait till I see that taxi stop in front of the house."

"I assume you're going to take some clothes up," William said.

"I'm going to borrow Nan's things. I don't like wearing the things you've bought for me."

"You're going to impose on them as totally as possible then."

"It's not an imposition," she said, rinsing out her glass. "Nan's my sister, and she's told me even before we got married I was in for some bad times with you." She turned the glass upside down next to the sink.

"In summation then," William said, "could we say you really don't know what you're doing or why you're doing it."

"Say what you want." She walked past him and into the living room.

"You don't suppose the onset of this month's cycle might in any way be . . ."

She stopped and turned around again. "I don't suppose it would. So please go swimming. Go do something." She finished speaking and walked to the window.

William watched her back for a few moments, then walked to the center of the room. "You mentioned the outing."

"I changed my mind," she said. "I don't see the point now."

"Would the mission be of any interest to you?"

"I don't think so."

"You said three days ago you wanted to see it."

"How far is it."

"Close."

"May I see on a map?"

He gestured toward the door. "There's one in the car."

Lisa didn't move.

"There's a map in the car, Lisa."

"Can't you bring it in?"

"Come out to the car," he said. "If the mission's close enough to get back in time for your taxi we'll go; otherwise we won't."

She waited a moment, then walked ahead of him out through the kitchen. William locked the door after him, and they walked out onto the driveway and to the car. He opened its door for her.

"I just want to see the map."

"Get in Lisa; we'll look at it."

She got in and he closed the door, then walked around to his side. Lisa opened the glove compartment and removed the map. William got in and started the engine.

"Bill." She reached for the door handle.

"I'm just warming it up."

"Turn it off."

He turned it off.

"You're trying to make me change my mind," she said, "but you can't." She opened the map.

"It's very close," William said.

She opened the map farther.

"You're looking up around San Francisco; maybe if you turned it over."

She turned it over.

"Shall I give you some help?"

"I can find it."

"You're looking on the desert now," he said. "Here." He pointed to a place on the map where the blue ocean stopped and the gray land started. "Right there; a little picture of a swallow shows where the mission is."

"And where are we."

He moved his finger up the coast.

"And how many miles is it."

"Very few."

She rested the map against the dashboard and moved her hand down to a corner of it. Holding her two fingers apart she measured a line indicating the number of miles to each inch, then moved her fingers up to the mission again. "It's far," she said.

"It's not."

"It's over twenty miles."

William shook his head. He measured the line at the corner of the page with his fingers, then moved it up to where his wife's hand was. "Eight or ten."

She put her fingers down to the corner again and brought them up. "Over twenty."

"Lisa, watch." He put his hand down to the corner. "Fifteen miles like this, right?" He opened his fingers a short distance.

"You shortened them as you came up."

"I didn't," he said. "Put your fingers with mine."

She held her two fingers open beside his.

"Now up."

They moved their hands slowly up to the mission again. "You see?" he said, putting them in place between the two points. "Less than fifteen."

"Not by the roads," she said. "You're doing it as the crow flies."

"Lisa," he said, putting his hand around hers.

"If you'd like to do something for an hour," she said, "fine. But I don't want to hold hands in the car."

He let go of her hand. "Let's drive," he said, turning on the ignition.

"But not to the mission."

He put the car into reverse and backed slowly out the driveway.

"Promise me we aren't going to the mission."

"I promise."

She folded her arms across her chest and looked out over the sea.

William turned up a short street, then stopped for a moment at a red light. "We'll just drive around a little to get rid of some of the tension." He jammed his foot down onto the floor and sped out onto the highway in front of a large diesel truck.

Without speaking they drove down the coast and through the town. There were long stretches of stucco apartment houses on the other side, then a housing development of ranch-style houses off to the right, and then open fields leading toward the cliff beside the sea. Lisa turned her head away from the window to look at her husband. "Where are we going."

"Just for a drive, Lisa." They turned around a curve. William glanced ahead at a large billboard beside the road. It pictured a mission bell and several swallows; underneath an arrow pointing ahead. He glanced again at his wife to see she hadn't noticed the sign.

"You're sure we aren't going to the mission," she said.

"What's that on the floor."

Lisa looked down at the floor.

"Do you see it?"

"What's what on the floor."

"An object of some kind," he said, "part way under the seat."

She leaned forward and looked down between her feet.

William glanced at the billboard as the car sped past it.

"An object?"

"It must have been nothing."

She looked back at her husband a few moments, then turned her face and looked out the window again. They drove down into a dip, then up again. "Where are we going," she said. "To the mission, aren't we."

"Who said we were doing that."

"Aren't we."

He gestured at the window. "Watch the scenery, Lisa; relax and look out at the clouds."

The street running along beside the mission was a shady one. Parking spaces were marked out in white lines leading out from the curb, a parking meter in front of each space. William drove past several parked cars, some of them with out-of-state license plates, then headed into an empty space. He turned off the ignition and removed the key from the switch, then reached over to the glove compartment, opened it and removed a camera. "I want to lock up," he said. "Could you get out first?"

His wife was looking out the window at an adobe wall of the mission.

William reached past her and pushed open her door. "Lisa?"

"I don't respect you, William."

"If you'll get out," he said, "I'll lock your door from the inside."

She continued looking ahead of her. "I don't . . ."

"I heard you," he said. "Now get out of the car so we can visit the mission." He waited a few minutes longer, then got out, closed his door and locked it. He walked around to the other side and held out his hand toward Lisa.

She shook her head.

A man and his wife stepped past William and opened the door of the car beside him. William walked up onto the sidewalk. He glanced at Lisa, facing off in another direction, then he looked down at the camera in his hand. He turned a knob till a number came into the small red window on the back. Then he held it up to his eye and aimed it at her. "Lisa?"

She didn't move.

"Do you think you could smile just for about two seconds while I take the picture? Just two seconds out of the two weeks? So at least we can fake it to the others when we get back?"

Her eyes stayed fixed on the parking meter in front of the car.

William clicked the camera. "Thanks; that'll be lots of fun to show around when we get back."

A station wagon turned into the empty space beside William's car.

"If you were rational," he said, walking back toward her, "if you had some understandable reason for wanting to go up to San Marino, that would be one thing; I'd probably help you."

"I have a reason."

Two small girls and a boy got out of the back of the station wagon and a father and mother out of the front.

"Tell me."

"I can't."

"Try."

"I have," she said. "I can't make you understand."

The family closed the doors of the station wagon and walked up onto the sidewalk, where the father deposited a coin in the parking meter.

"Lisa, if we have something to figure out, then let's start figuring it out." He cleared his throat. "Please don't go up there to your sister."

"I'm going."

"Is it last night? You said it wasn't last night."

"It's not."

"We haven't fought in our marriage, Lisa. Really. Now I'm asking you not to go up there."

She looked up at him.

"Please; or tell me what I've done."

"You've done nothing," she said, "but I want some time to think."

He took her wrist. "Think here," he said.

She removed her wrist from his hand.

"Is it that I don't leave you in peace enough?" He tried to take her wrist again but she moved it away.

"Bill."

"Your sister and I," he said, crouching down between the two cars and looking up at her, "have never gotten along. You'll humiliate me by going up and staying with them."

"I'm sorry."

"We'll talk about the marriage; that's at the root of it, isn't it. Have I failed. Where have I failed, Lisa."

"This is gibberish," she said. "You're a good husband; you do everything right, if that's what you want me to say. But I want to get off by myself and think about why I'm not happy."

He reached up to her leg. "I'll make you happy."

"You won't," she said. "I don't want you to. I want to figure out why I'm unhappy."

He squeezed her leg. "Please don't go to San Marino."

"William."

"Really." He patted her leg. "This plan of yours. It won't last." He squeezed her knee. "You're having a bad day. You're a little disoriented in the new environment at the beach; that's all. *Lisa, what have I done!*" The camera fell out of his hand onto the street. He didn't pick it up.

"I don't respect you."

"But can't we talk about it? Let's try."

There was a toothpick on the dashboard. Lisa picked it up, looked at it a moment, then placed it between her teeth.

"We got married a year and a half ago," William said.

"I'm just reviewing. I work hard. I . . ." He took her arm. "Lisa, please; this is humiliating for me."

"You're just babbling, Bill."

"Four days ago I invited Nan and Chester to come down to the beach some afternoon for a picnic. And now you're going to show up on their doorstep in a taxi? Asking them to pay your fare?"

"Yes."

"If you want peace, privacy, you can have it here. I'll move up to a motel on the highway. Okay?"

"No."

"I'll eat out."

She removed the toothpick from between her teeth and returned it to the dashboard.

"For the whole rest of the vacation you can have the house to yourself."

She leaned back in the seat, looking out at the peeling adobe wall on the other side of the sidewalk and at the branch of a pepper tree hanging over it.

"What am *I* supposed to do when you're in San Marino."

"About your cooking?"

"My rest. How can I relax with this happening. I'll be more keyed up when I get back to work than when I left."

She shrugged.

"Not to be maudlin, Lisa, but don't you care anything at all about me?"

"I don't know."

"Well isn't that the issue?" He cleared his throat. "We've never . . . we haven't actually talked about it, but our feelings about each other. What are they, Lisa."

"Bill," she said, staring straight ahead, "I don't have feelings. I go along; I get your food. On the weekends we see friends. I shop. I see my friends. We watch television at night, then we go to bed. Two or three nights a week we have sex together before we go to sleep." She shook her head. "I don't know if I was ever not numb, Bill, but in the last few days I've come to realize I'm numb, totally numb, from the top of my head down to my toes; so please don't make me keep talking."

William continued looking up at her while several people walked along the sidewalk past the front of the car. Finally he reached down and picked up the camera from beside the tire. "You're going to leave, aren't you."

"Yes."

"No matter what I say."

"That's right."

"Lisa?" He set the camera on the floor of the car. "If you could . . . maybe if you could tell me what to do . . . to make you . . ." he looked down at the pavement ". . . respect me."

"I don't know."

"Because I work," he said. "I make money; I have a good apartment for us." He clenched his fist. "I do what I . . . it seems like I do what's right. So . . ." He cleared his throat. "So what can I do *more.*"

"I don't know."

"You just don't respect me?"

"No."

"Have you ever?"

She sat quietly looking out at the adobe wall.

"Have you ever respected me, Lisa?"

"I don't think so."

"At first?"

"I don't think so."

"By why is this happening." He pushed his fist against the side of the car seat. "Do you know?"

"No."

"Can't we just go in and see the mission together? Enjoy it together? You're saying we can't do it?"

She didn't answer.

"I mean I can see we can't," he said. Two pigeons landed on top of the wall. "I can see it. I don't know why, but I see we can't." He waited a few moments longer, then slowly stood. "Respect."

She nodded.

"That's what it comes down to, isn't it. I mean I want to know."

"That's what it comes down to."

William stood beside the car for a long time, looking over its roof at a souvenir shop across the street. His wife sat quietly on the seat. There was a clanking sound as some visitors came through a turnstile at the entrance of the mission, then a taxi turned around the corner and drove up beside the curb. A man opened the back door and got out. He paid the driver through the window, then walked to the entrance of the mission.

William stepped out into the street, walked past several parked cars and bent down beside the open window of the cab. "My wife wants to go to San Marino."

The driver looked up at him.

"Would it be possible for you to take her there."

"Where is she."

William stepped aside and pointed down at their car.

The driver looked down at Lisa, then back at William. "It's eighty miles away," he said. "I'll have to clear it."

"Please clear it." William walked back to his car. "He's clearing it; I think he'll take you."

Lisa stepped out of the car and William closed the door for her. He walked along beside her behind the other cars and to the taxi. The driver finished speaking into a microphone on his dashboard, then looked out at William and nodded. William opened the back door of the cab and Lisa got in. "Goodbye, Lisa."

The driver reached back and slammed the door shut. He locked it, wrote something on a sheet of paper on a clipboard beside him on the seat, then released his hand brake and made a wide U-turn. William stood looking after him as the car headed down the street. When it had turned around a corner and disappeared he stepped up onto the curbing.

The adult admission was seventy-five cents. William paid it, accepted a small brochure in return for his ticket, then walked through an opening in the adobe wall. Inside a young Mexican girl walked up to him holding a tray of small plastic sacks. "Ten cents," she said.

"What is it."

"Corn."

William reached into his pocket for some change, removed two nickels from it and handed them to the girl. She gave him a sack of corn.

William carried the brochure and the small sack of corn to a bench. He seated himself; then he untied a knot in the top of the plastic bag. He reached in and removed several yellow grains. He tossed them down onto the ground. Three pigeons hurried over and began pecking at them, the last one being pushed aside by the others. William reached in for some more corn, lowered his hand near the third one and dropped it, watching as he began to eat. Then he tied a knot in the plastic sack again, set it on the bench and picked up the brochure. Beginning with the caption under the picture on the front he read each word from the beginning to the end. Then he fitted it into his pocket, picked up the corn and started down a path toward an old church.

About ten minutes later, in a garden at the far end of the mission grounds, William lost control of himself. He was standing beside a stone statue. Several feet away was a sundial. Clutching the bag of corn very tightly in his hand, he turned around and looked behind him, down the path, but no one was there. Then, suddenly, he lifted the bag up over his head and hurled it as hard as he could against the sundial, bursting the plastic and sending grains of corn flying into the air. Then he put his hands up over his face. He kept them there, his eyes closed tightly, till the birds began to come and peck at the grains on the gravel walk and on the sundial. Then he turned around and started walking back along the path, keeping his hands up over his face until he started to get near the crowded area, then keeping his face tipped down as he walked past the other visitors, so none of them would see he was crying, and then out the front and to his car again.

TWO

From eighth grade through twelfth grade William Alren had attended a boys' school in the hills behind Santa Barbara, called Midland. During his second year there the headmaster had written the following on the back of one of his reports:

> Bill still seems to have the problem in his mind which we've mentioned before, that is, that he always feels he has made the wrong decision. This is apparent most recently in the selection of his optional course—we spoke after dinner last week and he mentioned that he would have been happier in the Physics course, but that he knew he had to stick with Chemistry and try and make the best of it.

Nearly always he expresses the opinion that things would be going better for him if only he'd made some other choice. Even when there seems to be no reason for misgivings, he feels sure he's made a bad step.

Right off hand, I don't see any way of dealing with this, except the giving of encouragement, which doesn't really seem to work. Let us hope it's something he will grow out of in time.

When he was home for Christmas vacation that year, William saw the report one morning on his mother's desk. He read his grades, then turned it over and saw the comment on the back. He sat down and thought about it for a few minutes before returning the card to the desk. He knew it was true.

Three years later he was a freshman at the University of Colorado. He spent the year unhappily, wishing he had chosen another school. After a summer of thinking it over, he returned to his sophomore year to find things seemed no better for him, and then composed a letter to the dean of an eastern college, saying he felt he had been guided in his choice of college by factors such as parental pressure, rather than his true feelings, and asked if he could transfer.

He sent the letter off along with an application and had the administration office send a transcript of his grades back. (A special-delivery letter to the dean, inspired and written one midnight, followed the other material east. It stated that he considered this to be the most important decision of his life and told him why, which was that he felt in moving all the way across the country he would be making a meaningful and symbolic break with his past and this would indicate the entering of the fully mature stage of his life.)

Two things happened. The first thing was that his father, who had been going in and out of sanitariums since William was ten, unsuccessfully trying to be cured of alcoholism, got suddenly much worse than he had been before. William's mother called to say he probably would have to stay in the sanitarium all the time from then on because he'd gotten very drunk and tried to damage himself. (William knew she meant he'd tried to kill himself, but they never talked about it again and he never found out how or any of the circumstances.) William listened as his mother talked to him, then he informed her that he was transferring to Princeton. She was silent after hearing the news. After a few moments she told him that it was his own decision to make. She said it would make it much harder for her, psychologically, to have William three thousand miles away, rather than just one thousand, but she would try and accept his decision. He felt badly about the conversation afterwards and wished he'd never said anything about the change.

The second thing happened the next day, which was that William was rejected as a transfer student by Princeton. At the bottom of the letter of rejection the dean wrote a personal note saying that he had many times been to Colorado and was sure there was no more gorgeous place on earth to spend one's four years of undergraduate life. After getting the letter William called his mother, said he had been thinking things over, and that under the circumstances and the seriousness of his father's condition, he would give up his plan to go east. She said she was grateful.

William still thought about the East though, usually about how the people there were probably different, probably more interesting, and that he would be making better friends if he were back there. The several friends he had at Colorado were chemistry majors. Aside from the chemistry majors, most of the others seemed too loud to William. They made him nervous. The chemistry majors didn't make him nervous but it was most often when he was with them, having a cup of coffee, going to a movie, that he wished he was somewhere else.

William's own major subject at college was psychology, and he chose it because he thought it would help him to understand himself and the people around him better. Sometimes he felt it was helping him have more awareness of himself, but other times it seemed irrelevant to anything that was happening to him and most of the time he wondered what it would have been like if he had majored in history instead.

When William was a senior he met a girl named Anne Madden, who had just come to the university for her first year. About a week after she came to school, after a dance, they went to William's room, drank beer, and went to bed together. For the rest of the year they studied together and went to bed once every two or three weeks, usually after a dance.

Another girl at the university was named Madeline Frost. She was in most of William's psychology classes, but he had never spoken to her. He felt very nervous every time he saw her and considered her to be the most beautiful girl he had ever seen. Usually when he went to bed with Anne he would find himself wishing, about half way through, that she was Madeline Frost. He tried to make himself stop having these thoughts, but he couldn't, even though he was a psychology major.

Before leaving college William and Anne Madden decided to get married. They didn't tell anyone though, and didn't plan to till school was over. Then, on the very last day of his college career, William did the thing that he always regretted afterwards more than anything else he'd ever done.

The graduation ceremony was held in a large amphitheatre. There was no one there that William had invited, since the only person he had invited was his mother and at the last minute something more went wrong with his father at the sanitarium and she felt she shouldn't leave him. The Maddens had come from the small town in Wyoming where Anne was from to take her home, and she persuaded them, after introducing William and telling them about the marriage plans, to stay and see William graduate. After meeting them William went with the other members of his class to get his gown and put it on. He went through the ceremonial march and took his seat in one of the front rows of the amphitheatre, then walked up to get his diploma when it was his turn. As he was getting it he looked out across the crowd and saw Anne Madden's father standing up and taking a movie of him. Then, when it was all over and the minister finished saying a prayer for his class, William did the thing he regretted.

He got up quickly from his seat and walked around to the side of the amphitheatre and toward the back. Just once he looked up to see Anne waving at him. "We're over here!" she called. William took off his cap and rested it on one of the seats as he passed it, even though all the members of his class had been instructed to return the gowns and caps to the building where they had gotten them. Then he turned and went out an exit and started running. As he ran across a large grass area he unfastened his black gown and let it fall behind him on the grass. He ran faster and faster toward his room. When he got to it he went inside and picked up his suitcases and his lamp. He picked up some pens and pencils off his desk, put them in his pocket, then ran out the door and to his car. He threw in his belongings and jumped in after them. Then he started the car and drove as fast as he could out of the parking lot and down the street toward the highway.

There were long periods on the drive home when he talked to himself aloud, swearing at himself and talking to Anne, begging her to forgive him. At one place in Arizona he stopped the car in the middle of the highway, turned around and started back. He had gone less than a mile, though, when he drove in through a gas station, turned around again and continued toward home, telling himself in a loud voice that he was the most cowardly and despicable person who had ever been born.

However, he never married Anne Madden and never saw or heard from her again.

His first job was with a corporation that made fuselages and other airplane parts. The plant was in Hawthorne, California, about an hour's drive from his mother's house, and William worked in the personnel department. His mother felt he could be doing more important work after four years of college and a degree in psychology, but he told her he didn't really believe in psychology any more, and that till he felt his feet were more on the ground he wanted a secure job that didn't have too many risks, even though it might be boring. Also, he had heard people with psychology degrees were looked upon favorably by personnel departments. He found this to be true in Hawthorne.

On some occasions the company would send him driving out to the airport to meet someone's plane. He looked forward to these times the most. For the most part, though, his job was to ask applicants some questions about their background. Then, based on their previous experience and his evaluation of their personality, he recommended that they be hired or not hired. He almost always recommended that they be hired, and it was for this reason that he didn't last at the job.

On his second job he met Lisa. It was in San Francisco. After living eight months with his mother and his two younger sisters in Palos Verdes he decided there might be better job opportunities in the northern part of the state. He drove his car up, got a motel room in San Francisco and began looking the next morning for a job. Even though the corporation in Hawthorne let him go, they gave him a good reference, and with this, in addition to his psychology degree, he found a job in two days. It was with a commercial airline company and included a six-month training program. He only got through four months of the program and was never sure what the job was that he was working toward, but it was while he was in training that he met Lisa.

It wasn't romantic how they met, although afterwards William often wished it had been. There was a girl in the training program whom William had lunch with, along with some of the others, nearly every day. One day after lunch as they were walking back to the building where the training program was held the girl asked William if he'd like to have a date with a friend of hers. Before he could say anything she said she'd already told her friend about him and she was crazy to meet him, which seemed odd to William, since he hardly knew the girl in the training program, and she knew nothing about him that she could have passed on to her friend. However, he agreed to drive up to Mill Valley, where the girl lived, and take her out the next evening.

It was a Friday. He drove Lisa from her parents' house back into the city to a movie, then back up to the house again, then home again himself. Altogether he figured out he had driven over ninety miles on the date.

She talked some of the time about her friend at the training program, how they had known each other since high school, and some of the time she talked about how she hated living at home. When he took her back they parked in front of the parents' house, kissed in the car for about half an hour, then William asked her if she was doing anything the next day. When she said she wasn't he asked if he could come up and take her for a drive. He came the next morning. They drove up in some hills behind Mill Valley. They kissed for a while in the back seat, then took off their clothes and had sex together.

For a long time William had been thinking his life would be easier if he were married, so he asked Lisa. She said she'd have to see, but before he took her home that evening she said she would. There was only one condition, and that was that they wouldn't live anywhere near San Francisco, since she had grown up there and hated it. She had a sister and brother-in-law in San Marino and hoped they could live somewhere down there, near them, because she knew William would quickly become good friends with Nan and Chester. William mentioned that he was in the middle of a training program. Lisa said she thought jobs were easy to get if you had an education. William had found this to be true, so he married her in a church near her parents' house, took a short honeymoon with her, then returned to Southern California, a place he had left just three and a half months before, thinking it would be for good.

Nan Morris came unexpectedly to the beach the day after Lisa left. She came just at noon. William had been on the beach during the morning, but when Nan came he was in the kitchen, a towel wrapped around his waist over his bathing suit, standing at the stove emptying a can of stew into a pan.

"I want to help," Nan said from behind him, "in any way I can."

William turned around to see his sister-in-law standing in the doorway between the kitchen and the outside patio.

"Hello, Bill."

"I didn't see you." He set the can down on the stove.

"I almost didn't come," Nan said, stepping into the kitchen, "then I realized at a time like this there really isn't any choice."

"Let's see," William said. "I'm just fixing some stew; would you like some?"

"No thank you."

William nodded. He rested his hands on his hips. "Did you bring your suit—would you like a swim."

"Thank you," she said. "I think I won't."

It was quiet a few moments.

"Well how is she then," he said finally. "How's Lisa."

"Bill," she said, removing one of her white gloves, "she's very worried, I'm very worried, and I want to help you save your marriage."

William looked down at the floor.

"I want you to let me," she said as she took off the other glove. "Even though we haven't been close before, I want you to let me, because it's now come clear that you and Lisa need some outside help."

William nodded.

"Now I know Lisa's desires, her needs. I'm probably more sensitive to her than anyone else in the world. So will you let me help the two of you save your life together."

William turned and walked back to the stove.

"Will you, Bill."

"What did she say. Have you talked?"

"We talked all night."

"Could I ask what about?"

"Everything," she said. "The problems of two people trying to build their future together, everything. We just talked as two sisters and two human beings."

William looked down at his stew for a few moments, then nodded. "Well, thank you for coming down."

"Don't thank me."

"I do thank you," he said, "and I thank you for offering your help."

"Accept it, Bill."

"I'd like to accept it." He turned and looked at her. "Why didn't Lisa come."

"She's not herself yet."

"She just didn't . . ."

"Bill," she said, putting the gloves into her purse as she took a step toward him, "you're both so very young, both still in your twenties. And there's still so much you have to learn about sharing in a marriage."

William turned back to the stew.

"So the first thing I want to suggest," Nan said, "is for the two of you to open a dialogue. From what Lisa says there's no dialogue in your marriage and I think that's probably the central tragedy."

William picked up a spoon from the stove and began stirring the stew.

"I'll sit out in the sun," Nan said, stepping back out onto the patio. "You fix your stew and bring it out." She walked over to a green cloth-covered swing against one of the walls, seated herself in the center of it, crossed her legs and began slowly to swing forward and backward, turning her head to look up at the overhanging branch of a eucalyptus tree as she swayed.

William walked to the cupboard and removed a plate, then carried it back to the stove.

"Bill? Can you talk out here while your meal is warming?" She pointed at an aluminum chair. "Why don't you sit down while it's warming. Did you have to prepare something else?"

"No." He stepped out into the sun. "Just a glass of milk." He seated himself on the chair which Nan had pointed to.

Nan glanced at a small gold watch on her wrist. "I don't want to stay any longer than I have to," she said, "so why don't we start in."

William reached down to remove a eucalyptus leaf stuck to his heel. "Start in how."

"Just start," she said.

He brought the leaf up to his lap and bent it slowly in half.

"Do you have any comments to begin with?"

William shook his head.

"None?"

He bent the leaf in another place. "What aspect of the marriage would you like to talk about."

"Bill," she said, moving forward on the swing, "I came here because I think I have the overview on your problems to help."

"You said that." He pulled the stem off the leaf. "So if you want an opening comment from me, I'll say this: I'm very tired from the amount of work I've done over the past few weeks."

"You need help, Bill."

"Excuse me just a minute." William got up, walked in the house and to the stove. He stirred the stew, then walked back outside and sat down again in the chair. "I appreciate your concern, Nan, but . . ."

"Do you feel you need help," she said, "or do you feel you don't need help."

"What kind of help do you think you can give us."

Nan rested her arms along the back of the swing and began swaying backward and forward again. For a few moments it was quiet, then she said, "Lisa told me what her immediate reason for leaving you was."

William looked up.

"You know, of course."

He shook his head.

"I'm sure you must know," she said, swinging slightly faster. "The incident the night before she left where she observed you spying on some girls on the beach."

William returned his gaze to a flagstone. For a few moments he studied the stone, then he cleared his throat. "Yes," he said. "That was a . . . I'm not proud of that, but we did bring it up, I apologized, and Lisa mentioned that it wasn't actually the reason for her leaving."

"She may have said that to you," Nan said, looking up at the fringe of the canopy over the swing, "but of course it was a terrific blow to her to have it happen. Certainly there's no need to go into the incident, but to clear the air I should tell you that Lisa related to me in detail your . . . what would you call it, your weakness, your peeping; whatever you choose to call it, she did give me an account of what's been going on since the two of you were married."

Again William looked up at her.

"I think you know what I'm talking about."

"Peeping?"

"What would you call it." Nan bent forward to pick up her purse from the ground, opened it and removed a package of cigarettes.

"Peeping?"

"We both know what I'm referring to."

"Something besides the other night?"

She found a match in her purse and lit the cigarette. "Please, Bill." She dropped the match and cigarettes back into the purse.

"Peeping?"

"Just to name one occurrence," she said, "maybe you

can think back to an incident in your apartment two or three months ago."

"The secretary?" William said.

"Yes."

"In the apartment below ours."

Nan nodded. "We're talking about the same incident," she said. "By the way, your stew is going over the side of the pan."

William got up and walked quickly back into the kitchen. He lifted the pan off the stove, stood a moment looking down at stew sizzling in the burner, then poured some of it onto the plate. He set a fork on the plate and carried it back to the patio.

"Let me ask you this," Nan said, "have you ever talked the incident in the apartment over with a doctor."

"No, Nan."

"I think you should."

There was a wooden table covered by a green and white sun umbrella in the center of the patio. William carried his plate to it and set it down. Then he sat and spread the stew out on the plate with the fork.

"William."

"Why do you bring it up; what about it."

She took another drag from the cigarette. "Do you know what I would do to Chester if I caught him doing what Lisa caught you doing in your apartment?"

"To be quite honest," William said spearing a piece of carrot, "I'd hate to think."

"Well I don't know what I'd do," she said, "and I don't want to think either. Let's just say Lisa showed a much greater degree of tolerance than I would have."

William rested his fork on the side of the plate. "What did Lisa say I did."

"We're talking about the same incident."

"I don't think we are."

"You tell me what you did."

He looked down at the plate.

"Can you?"

"In my mind," William said, "the incident doesn't

merit the attention we're giving it."

Nan settled back in her seat. "Maybe Lisa misrepresented it."

"She may have," William said. "Perhaps I could go over it very quickly and clear it up."

"Do."

William rested his hands in his lap and looked down at the table. "As I recall," he said, "it was a Saturday night."

Nan nodded.

"I don't remember exactly what Lisa was doing at the time," he said. "I think she was working on a dress, sewing on it in the bedroom."

"That was her remembrance too."

William nodded. "As I recall I was in the living room watching a television program. I'd been watching it for an hour or so." He looked up at Nan. "Does that . . ."

"That checks out."

He looked back down at the table. "Now what I did," he said, "that seems to be causing the distress, was to go into the bathroom, get the mirror, the little hand mirror, and then go to the closet and get three wire hangers. I straightened out the three wire hangers, made a hook in the end of each length of wire, and hooked them all together into a long piece. Right?"

"Lisa didn't go into quite as much detail. Right."

"After that," William said, "I fastened the end piece of wire around the handle of the mirror. And now we come to the part that probably is upsetting."

Nan looked down at the point of her shoe.

"Having earlier, during a commercial, heard water running in a bathtub somewhere below our living room, it occurred to me that probably someone was taking a bath. Realizing a girl who is a secretary lived in that apartment, it seemed a strong possibility that I could guess who it would be taking a bath. So after fixing the mirror to the end of the hangers, I opened the window beside the chair where I'd been watching television and lowered the mirror down along the side of the apartment house toward a window below."

"And what did you see."

"Hardly anything."

"You saw the secretary taking a bath," she said, "didn't you."

"I'm not sure."

Nan held up her cigarette. "Where shall I put this out."

"On the cement."

She set it down on the cement in front of the swing and ground it out with her shoe.

"If it was her," William said, "I saw her for about three seconds. The blind was drawn over the window. I had to lower the mirror down just between the level of the top of the window and where the top of the blind was. This took a number of minutes, maneuvering it into place, in addition to which the mirror was jiggling on the end."

Nan bent forward for a new cigarette.

"And that was that. Lisa came in: I was a little embarrassed; I told her what I was doing, and that ended it."

"You saw the secretary naked, in other words."

"Yes, Nan. For about two seconds in a jiggling mirror."

Nan put the cigarette in her mouth and lit it. "But you saw her breasts, the rest of her."

"I don't know what I saw. It might have been a breast, it might have been the handle of a water faucet—the whole thing was unsuccessful. But why blow it up, why even mention it."

She began swinging gently forward and backward in the swing. "What do you feel about it now," she said.

"The incident?"

"What's your attitude."

"I feel embarrassed. I'm embarrassed that Lisa came in and caught me; I'm embarrassed that she told you."

"And that's all?"

"I feel sheepish, I feel very embarrassed. What do you want."

"Not ashamed though."

"Ashamed."

"But you don't want to admit there's something wrong with your psychological balance."

William shook his head.

"You don't."

He picked up his fork, loaded it with a piece of beef and an onion and put them in his mouth. "It's a little bit . . . it's immature, trying to get kicks that way. It's maybe a teenage holdover—I should be past things like that. But I'm not . . . there's no deep psychological . . ."

"There's not."

"No, Nan."

"You're sure about that."

"I might have problems of one kind or another, but they don't get the best of me."

"And what about the magazines, Bill."

He looked up.

"You know which ones I mean," she said, smiling.

"You mean the . . ."

She nodded.

"Lisa . . . you must have talked quite a while."

"Most of the night."

William shrugged. "Occasionally I get the urge to buy one of them and I get one and bring it back home and look at it."

"Do you know why?"

"I don't know why."

"Does it give you a fulfillment that sexual union with your wife doesn't give you?"

William speared a large bite of potato. "Let's get off this subject," he said, raising it to his mouth.

"Bill," she said, "let's get one thing straight. Chester's been known to buy men's magazines, ones with good-quality fiction, sophisticated jokes. I can't say I'm happy about his having them, but I realize that kind of magazine is widespread, it has a certain respectability and I can accept it. But the kind you buy aren't widespread."

"Maybe more than you might . . ."

"They're confined to a certain type of person," she said, "and that's why this is so disturbing; because you're not, at least I don't think you are, that kind of person."

He scraped the remaining stew toward the center of his plate. "These magazines that we're referring to."

"Let's be sure we're . . ."

"Right."

"I'm referring to magazines with pictures of nude women in them, embracing each other, kissing each other, and other things."

William raised more stew to his mouth. "They have laws about showing the other things—it's just the first two."

"You seem to be an authority."

"I'm not." He put the stew in his mouth. "I'm not an authority and I'm not obsessed. A couple times I brought home a magazine such as you've described. I looked at it; I was curious. I found it to be mildly titillating I will confess. As far as its being an indication of some deep distorted passions lurking under my surface, I think this isn't a justified conclusion. However, since you bring it up, I assure you I will keep on the constant alert for signs of any kind of moral decay as I go along. I ask you to entrust this job to me." He scooped up some more stew.

"And the movie?" Nan said. "You went to that movie, didn't you. The theatre over by . . ."

"The Oaks."

"And then you came home and boasted to Lisa about going to it."

"I didn't boast to Lisa about it," he said. "I went to it. I came back home. She asked me where I'd been and I said I'd gone to that movie."

"All afternoon."

"Yes, Nan," he said. "If you want to know, I was in an aimless mood that day, the market was down, I thought it might help get my mind off the decline a little to see the nude movies."

"And did you feel better afterwards?"

William glanced at the aluminum pole that rose up through the center of the table and supported the umbrella over his head. "Yes."

"You did."

"It seemed to have a good effect on my spirits—I wouldn't know why exactly."

"But it made Lisa cry," she said, "didn't it."

"Yes."

"Could I ask what she did when you told her you'd been to it?"

"She gave me a strange look and said something about wasting my money." He lifted more stew to his mouth.

"Last night when she was telling me about it," Nan said, "she was crying."

"I'm sure she was; I feel like crying myself."

"Why."

"Because you're a depressing person." He stood and lifted up his plate.

"Sit down, Bill."

"I'm through."

"Please," she said, "just sit down another minute."

He started toward the house. "I have an urge," he said, "which you might call lascivious. It's controllable, but it's an urge. I've always had it. I went to a boys' school, no social life, maybe that's where I picked it up, maybe before. But I realize it. Being married makes it seem like I shouldn't have it any more, but the fact is I do."

"Lisa said on your honeymoon you came back to your motel room and told her you saw a nude woman through one of the other windows."

"That's right, Nan."

"It is."

"It was an accident," he said. "A fortunate accident, I would call it. But it's true I saw a nude woman in the window at the end of the motel and mentioned it to Lisa."

"On the first night of your honeymoon."

"Second night."

"And did Lisa express any emotion when you mentioned it to her?"

William looked down at a flagstone. "I tried to present it in a restrained manner."

"But did she show any emotion."

William let his eyes stay a few more moments on the flagstone, then nodded. "Yes."

"Oh?"

"She got upset; she cried."

Nan took another drag from her cigarette.

"But she got over it," he said. "I explained it was an accident; that was that."

Nan motioned him back toward his bench. "Sit, Bill."

"In a way," he said, walking slowly back with his empty plate and stopping beside the table, "you could even say it was like a hobby."

"What's that."

"This urge," he said, seating himself. "I mean it's sort of come to be like my hobby." He looked up at her. "Does Chester have a hobby?"

"He works out in the garden."

"There," William said, "you see, he has one too."

Nan finished her cigarette, ground it out with the toe of her shoe, then got up from the swing. There was a window beside the kitchen door. She stepped in front of it to see her reflection, then straightened the front of her suit slightly. When she was finished she turned around again. "Isn't there a little path along the cliff up there?" she said, pointing up toward the driveway. "You have such a breathtaking setting here; I'd just like to stretch my legs before I go."

William walked to the door of the kitchen and set his plate inside on a table. "There's a short trail up there," he said, "if you'd want to walk along it."

"Will you come along?"

"Sure."

She put her hands behind her, locking her fingers, and started up toward the street. "You say you've always had this fascination," she said.

"What's that."

"The magazines," she said. "The looking in windows."

William caught up to her. "That's one way to look at it. Another way to look at it is that I've just happened to be in the right places at the right times, sometimes."

They reached the street. "Which way."

William pointed.

"The magazines," she said, starting in the direction he'd pointed. "What sort of . . . feeling do you get looking at them."

"I don't know. Just . . . kind of a curiosity about the girls."

"Their bodies."

"That's part of it." They stepped closer to the side of the road as a car passed. "Sometimes I wonder about the background of the girls, if they went to school, what town they might be from, what their aspirations might be. Usually the pictures of them are taken in bedrooms, although one article was all taken with three girls doing different things with each other in a kitchen. I wonder whose house it might be; if the girls are married—once I noticed a light ring around one of their wedding ring fingers, so she must have taken off her ring for the pictures. Sometimes they have a picture on their wall, or a radio on a table, or a certain style of lamp. You can tell things about them by these."

They came to the edge of a vacant lot and to a trail that led through the brown grass to the cliff, houses on each side of the trail. "Have you always had this obsession?"

"It's not an obsession."

Nan walked ahead, keeping her fingers locked behind her. "But you've always enjoyed looking at naked women."

"Why lie about it."

Nan reached the end of the trail, then rested her hand

on a low wooden fence and looked out at the sea.

"That's the main beach down there," William said, pointing at it.

"Oh yes."

They stood looking down the coastline for a few moments. "You know, this isn't really as important a part of my life as it sounds."

"It's just your hobby."

"That's all."

"And you're actually being quite serious when you say your hobby is looking at naked women."

William put his hands in his pockets. "If there's one around I'll look at her. If not, I won't really go out and find one. It's just a part-time hobby." He looked down at a man and a woman lying on the sand at the base of the cliff.

Nan tossed her head so the wind blew through her hair. "Do you have the urge right now?"

"Not really," he said. "I mean it's always there, sort of waiting for an opportunity."

Nan turned and pointed at one of the houses on the opposite side of the cliff. "What if you saw one in that window over there."

William looked over at it.

"What would you do," she said, "if you saw a naked woman in that window."

"I'd look at her."

"You would."

"Sure."

"Without feeling at all ashamed?"

"Oh I'd feel ashamed," he said. "I'd say that's the main drawback of this particular hobby, feeling ashamed. But I'd look around to be sure no one was watching me looking at her; then I'd look at her."

"Would you feel lustful?"

"No," he said, "I'd just look."

"In other words," Nan said, turning to face him, "you're in the mood right now to see a nude woman."

William bent over and picked up a small stone. He

tossed it out over the cliff and watched it fall onto the beach below.

"Are you?"

"I told you," he said. "When the opportunity's there . . ."

"Let me ask you this," she said. "Just hypothetically." She cleared her throat. "Not that it could ever . . . but let's just . . . take myself, hypothetically. Just so I can try and understand this problem of yours better. Say the opportunity . . . what if you saw me in that window over there."

They looked over at the window.

"Unclothed, you mean."

"Yes."

He continued looking over at the window. "What if I did," he said.

"Would you still look if it was me?"

"I don't know," he said. "I don't know if I could tell it was you at this distance."

"But if you could."

William shrugged. "I guess I'd wonder what you were doing over in that house."

"But would you look at me."

"I don't know," he said, "I mean if the situation arose that you were over in that window and I was here and I saw you over there, then I'd have to make the decision of whether to look at you or not at that time."

"What if I ask you to look at me," she said.

He looked down at the ground.

"I hope you realize I never would think of a thing like this," she said, "but what if I asked you to come back to your house and look at me."

"Let's see."

"Would you?"

"Without your things on."

"If we went back and into the house and I took my clothes off. Would you look at me."

William reached up to touch his hand against his chin. "No."

"You wouldn't?"

"No."

"Why not."

"It would be an odd thing to do. It would be too personal if it was someone I knew, besides Lisa."

Nan nodded. "I just wanted to see what you'd say," she said. "I wanted to make sure you weren't as far gone as I thought you might be."

William bent over for another stone. He hurled it off over the ocean, then they started back along the path.

THREE

When she was thirteen Lisa had temper tantrums. They usually happened at dinner. When they occurred Lisa would get up from the table, yelling at the others, let her chair fall down behind her, then run across the room, dropping her napkin on the rug, and down the hall to the bathroom. She would slam the door, sometimes more than once, then lock it and sink down onto her knees on a thick blue rug. She would cry for half an hour, sometimes an hour. Once she picked up a hand mirror and hurled it at the mirror over the sink, breaking both of them. Another time she picked the porcelain cover up off the tank of the toilet and smashed it in the bathtub.

She wasn't punished for her tantrums. After the click of the lock in the bathroom door her mother would ask either her father or older brother to pick up Lisa's napkin from the floor. One of them would get up, retrieve the napkin and carry it back to the table. Later, after Nan had carried off the plates and brought in dessert, Mrs. Hamil might ask one of her children to go to the bathroom door and tell Lisa her dessert was on the table. Usually when this happened Lisa screamed and pounded on the door with her fists until the person returned to the table. When he had finished his own dessert, Lisa's younger brother would ask his mother if he could eat Lisa's. She would then call down the hall to tell Lisa she was giving her dessert to her brother; there would be a new burst of screaming, and Mrs. Hamil would nod to her son that it was all right if he ate his sister's dessert.

Usually Lisa cried until she was tired out. She would leave the bathroom, walk quietly past her parents in the living room, where they would be reading or watching television, and into her room, where she would close the door, lock it and go to bed.

One tantrum was brought on by her mother telling her she couldn't go out in a boy's car, and another by her mother telling her she had to go to her grandmother's birthday party. Although they were all for separate reasons, it was always her mother who caused them. At first Lisa would ask her father if he thought it was fair what she was being told to do. But after he had expressed the opinion several times that her mother always knew the best thing to do, Lisa learned not to ask his help any more but to start screaming instead. Sometimes it worked and Lisa got what she wanted, but usually it didn't.

On her third day in San Marino, sometime in the early morning, Lisa nearly had her first tantrum since she was thirteen. Nan had given her two sleeping pills the night before. She slept several hours, but around four in the morning her eyes came open in the darkness and she was suddenly fully awake.

She lay awhile on her back, looking up into the dark toward the ceiling. Slowly she began thinking about William. She turned over on her side and closed her eyes. She lay without moving for several minutes, then turned over the other way. Half an hour passed. Finally she got up, felt her way to the bathroom and turned on the light. She took a drink of water, stood looking at her reflection a few moments, then turned off the light and found her way back to bed.

It was an hour later that she thought she might not be able to remain quiet. She was lying on her stomach with her arms around the pillow and her face buried in it. She had cried for most of the hour and while crying she had developed a headache. Sometimes she bit her lip to keep from crying loudly. Once she got up and stepped out into the hallway. She stood a long time on the carpet between the door of her bedroom and the door of her sister and brother-in-law's bedroom, trying to decide whether or not to try and go into their bathroom for another pill. Finally she stepped back into her own room, closed the door and walked to the bed again. She knelt down beside it, put her forehead against the edge of the mattress and stayed that way, weeping quietly part of the time, and part of the time just staring ahead of her at the sheet, till the sun rose outside, turning the room slowly from black to gray.

By breakfast she had made a decision. Sitting across from her sister at the table, she announced it: "About going down to the beach today," she said, "if you want to drive me down, fine, I'd appreciate it; but otherwise I'll find a way down myself. I want to go down and stay with William, not just go down and get my clothes, as we planned."

Nan reached out for Lisa's juice glass.

"I'm sorry," Lisa said.

"Don't be sorry."

"But I'm sorry to have involved you and Chester in all this."

Nan got up and carried the empty glass to the sink. "Don't think of us," she said, turning on the water, "just do what you think's best."

"I'm trying to."

"You were up a large part of the night, weren't you; crying."

"Yes."

"You still really don't know what to do, do you."

"No."

Nan opened a cupboard for a bowl, then lifted down a box of cold cereal. "And that's why you came up here, isn't it, because you didn't know what else to do."

"I don't know why I came up here, Nan."

Nan got a carton of milk from the refrigerator and poured some of it on the cereal. "We're going down there to get your clothes this morning, Lisa, because that's what's best. And I want you to promise me you'll get the clothes and come right back." She set the cereal down in front of her. "Promise me you won't let him draw you into an argument." She walked across the room for a spoon and carried it to her sister. "Will you do that?"

"I don't know."

"Promise me you won't let him entice you to stay, Lisa." She removed the top of a small sugar bowl, spooned out some sugar and sprinkled it on Lisa's cereal. "There." She handed her a spoon.

"Thank you."

Nan glanced at her watch. "We'll get started as soon as you're ready." She walked across the kitchen and out the door, but then stepped back through. "You're coming to some conclusions on your own, Lisa," she said, "about life, about people. The minute you climbed in the taxi and told him to take you to San Marino you became a woman, I don't know any other way to say it." She raised a hand toward her sister. "So don't fall back now. Don't let him, don't let anyone talk you out of what you're doing, where you're going; don't let him pull you back to where he had you before." She lowered her hand. "Don't."

Lisa shook her head.

"Promise me you won't let him pull you down into the mire again."

"I won't let him pull me down into the mire again."

"Good. We'll go when you're ready." She left the room.

Lisa looked down into her puffed wheat for a few moments, then pressed the surface of the dry kernels down under the level of the milk and began to eat.

Nan talked most of the way down, sometimes interrupting herself to honk at another driver on the freeway, but mostly talking about her life with Chester and how it had taken Chester several years to realize that the only way to have a successful marriage is to let the wife have an equal voice in all the decisions. Lisa sat on the other side of the seat, listening. As they were passing some orange groves Nan made the comment that Chester had once actually broken down and cried in front of her, and that it had been very hard for her to do, but that she had ignored him at first and then told him to stand up and act like a man.

"What was he crying about," Lisa said.

"I don't remember."

"Did he hurt himself?"

"Oh no," she said, moving into the center lane to pass a slower car in front of them, "it was some emotional problem."

"And you don't remember what it was."

She moved back into the other lane. "Yes, I remember," she said. "It was the time his father died." She honked and sped past a slower car. "But you don't break down and cry in front of your wife. Of course you're upset when your father dies, but you don't dissolve into tears over it—you carry your grief like a man. And he learned that. With my help I think he came to realize we live in a world where the strong hold sway. Men don't cry. At least not a man I would marry. I think he came to see that and I think that was the turning point in the marriage when he did. Before that he was sort of a jelly donut, you won't tell anyone I ever said that of course, but after I told him I wouldn't cater to his whims any more he straightened up and I think he's turned into a man now, a real one." She pressed her hand on the horn again. In front of them a man in a pick-up truck swerved out of the way as she sped past. "You have to discover that they just simply cannot cope for themselves, Lisa, regardless of what they tell you."

"You mean men," Lisa said.

"Yes."

When they got to the beach house William was in the chair by the front window, looking out at the ocean. Nan walked into the room first. "Don't get up, Bill," Nan said as she walked into the room.

William turned, then began rising from his chair.

"Don't get up," Lisa said.

He stopped.

"Really," she said.

He lowered himself back down onto the chair.

Nan stopped in the center of the room, opened her purse and pulled out an orange one-piece bathing suit. "I brought this today," she said.

William looked at the suit.

"I hope it's all right," she said. "If you . . ."

"Fine." William gestured out toward the ocean. "Help yourself."

"There's a dressing room downstairs," Lisa said, "or you can change in our bedroom."

Nan pointed up the stairs. "Is the bedroom . . .?"

"Yes."

"I'll go up there." She walked to the stairs and started up.

William opened a newspaper on his lap, but his eyes stayed fixed on a photograph at one side.

It was quiet a few moments, then Lisa seated herself in the corner. She picked up the book she had been reading three nights before, looked at its title a moment, then set it down again. "I just came for my clothes," she said. "I don't know if there's anything you want to say; if not, I'll pack."

William didn't look up.

After a few more moments Lisa stood. "I'll pack," she said, "unless you can think of anything to say about us or about the separation."

William nodded at her chair. "Sit down."

She seated herself.

He looked up into her eyes. "Is separation the new word for it?"

"I don't think it's new."

"I didn't hear it the other day."

She shrugged.

"I just want to be sure I have the right terminology in mind."

Lisa glanced at her watch. "If you want to have a talk about an understanding," she said, "fine. If not . . ."

"Understanding."

"Yes," she said. "Does that word cause you problems too?"

"Just let me fit it into my working vocabulary."

Lisa began getting up from the chair again. "I thought you'd want to talk," she said. "If not, I'll pack."

William rested the newspaper on one of his knees. "I do, Lisa."

"Then don't pretend you don't understand me."

"Sit down."

She settled back on the chair.

"I'd like very much to talk," he said. "Is there something you'd like to say to begin?"

"It seemed we might talk about an arrangement."

"Arrangement," he said. "Go ahead."

"Speaking financially," Lisa said, "Chester and Nan have agreed to pay my meals and side expenses for the time being. But I hope you'll give me fifty or sixty dollars a month to help out; you don't have to, of course."

"A month?"

"Does that seem unreasonable?"

"You plan to be there on a monthly basis?"

"They've offered to have me there on a monthly basis," she said. "If it works out that way would you want to help with my expenses?"

"No."

"You wouldn't."

"No." William dropped his paper on the floor. "That's very kind of them, isn't it."

"Do you want to talk?" his wife said, looking up at him, "because if you just want to make sarcasms, I'll pack."

"I don't want to talk about Chester and Nan's generosity," he said, "because it's something that doesn't exist."

"That's your opinion."

"It's not," he said. "It's not my opinion that they like keeping us split up as long as they can—because it helps keep their minds off their own misery." He looked up at the sound of footsteps on the stairs.

Holding a towel and a bathing cap, dressed in her bathing suit and a pair of sandals, Nan stepped down into the living room. "Anyone else coming?" She stood looking at William. "Bill? A swim?"

"No."

"It looks like you could use some exercise." She walked past him to the door. "You be all packed when I come up, Lisa. We have to start right back." She glanced over at William and smiled. "We left Mark at one of the neighbors," she said. Then she walked out the door and started down the steps toward the beach.

"You're not in a mood to talk," Lisa said, "are you."

"I was, I think, till you came."

Lisa got up, walked across the room and up the stairs.

William turned his face toward the window. Below, Nan walked out over the beach. She spread her towel on the sand, then seated herself and reached into the bathing cap for a package of cigarettes.

William looked at the stairs. "Lisa?"

There was no answer.

He waited a moment, then got up and walked to the foot of the stairs. "Lisa."

"I'm packing, Bill."

He started up the stairs and stopped at the top beside

the bedroom door. He leaned against the wall, glancing at the chair in the corner where Nan had draped her dress and slip, then at his wife.

Lisa's suitcase was open on the bed and she was laying a green dress in on top of it.

"Don't tell me I'm not in a mood to talk, Lisa. I am in a mood to talk."

"You're in a mood to argue."

"No." He crossed his arms over his chest. "Just one somewhat unpleasant thing that I feel should be brought up," he said, "then we can go on to other things."

"What's that."

"I don't know how to say it exactly, except that Nan tells me you two have had some good conversations together."

Lisa stopped smoothing the dress, but her eyes remained fixed on it. "Yes?" She walked to the closet for a pair of high-heeled shoes.

"Some intimate sister-to-sister conversations."

She set the shoes in the suitcase on her dress.

"You didn't learn anything good about Chester, did you. Any tidbits you could tell me to make up for some of the tidbits Nan got about me."

Lisa walked to the closet and removed a skirt from a wire hanger.

"Do you know what I'm talking about, Lisa?"

"Yes."

"Tell me."

"The sex magazines. Spying."

"Right. And since when has it become a major issue, a major problem in your mind."

She carried the skirt to the suitcase. "If there are things you want kept secret," she said, setting it in, "I guess you should be more discreet about them."

"I guess so."

"Do you want to talk about our arrangement?"

"No."

"Then it would be easier for me to pack if you went back downstairs."

The sunlight was slanting in across the bed and across part of the open suitcase. William walked slowly to the window. He stood looking down at Nan as she strode toward the water. When she reached it she let a wave roll up over her feet. Then she dropped her cigarette on the sand. She pulled the bathing cap over her head, tucking her hair in under the side of it. "The arrangement," William said, watching as his sister-in-law, far below, buttoned the rubber strap of the bathing cap under her chin. "Let's discuss it."

"It's very simple, Bill. I'll live there till we either come to an understanding or we don't."

William nodded.

"I'll keep living there after you go back to work. That part's clear, isn't it."

"When you talked about months," he said, "it became clear."

"You could come over," she said, "maybe in the evenings. We could discuss things for an hour or so every evening, if that wouldn't inconvenience you."

William looked down at a dead spider on the window sill. "It shouldn't tax me too much."

"Nan's talked to a doctor she'd heard of, who might be of some help to us."

William nodded.

"I haven't met him yet. I have an appointment with him at three this afternoon; that's another reason we have to start back."

"What kind of doctor."

"A psychiatrist," Lisa said. "He specializes in marriage problems."

"You're brainwashed, aren't you. After two days." William looked back up and through the window. Nan was out to her waist in the ocean. She jumped up, holding her arms to the sides, as a wave rolled in past her.

"I don't know what the doctor charges," Lisa said, laying a blouse into the suitcase. "We can work that out. I won't let Nan pay for that, even if she offers."

"What if we don't reach an understanding," William

said. He watched Nan dive through a wave, come up and wipe water out of her eyes.

"I don't know. There's no reason to be pessimistic."

"I'm sure there's not," he said, "but shouldn't we slip the word 'divorce' in along with all the others before going too much farther?"

"I don't see why."

"Because that's what Nan's working on," he said. "I hope you see that—I hope you're not that far gone."

Lisa opened a drawer in the chest of drawers. "Someone on their street is a divorce lawyer. They think he would be a good one to get in touch with if it comes to that."

"They do."

"Yes," she said, "but to say they want us to get divorced isn't showing a firm grasp on reality."

"You think it's imagination that your sister might have ulterior motives."

"I do."

"Then I'll just say this." He took a step forward. "This is just a game, Lisa."

"What is."

"People who talk like this—divorce, arrangement—are just playing games with each other because they're too bored, too dull to think of anything better to do. But we aren't like that, Lisa. Leave the games to Chester and Nan."

"Excuse me." She walked past him.

He watched her go to the bureau and open its top drawer. "You have a very nice life up there, don't you."

She lifted up several pairs of underpants and carried them to the suitcase.

"Nice and comfortable," he said. "Secure. No decisions to make for yourself any more."

She carried a bra to the bed.

"No thinking required. No problems to solve. Just pablum all day and night from Nan and Chester."

"You see," she said, looking up at him, "this is what

I finally decided I didn't want any more of."

"Thinking, you mean."

"No," she said. "The pressure, the nagging, the demanding."

"I'm demanding that you think, Lisa."

She dropped the bra in the suitcase. "You're just demanding. It's your nature to demand; maybe some people wouldn't mind it. I do though." She walked back to the closet.

William lifted up the suitcase from the bed.

"What are you doing."

"Putting this down." He set it on the floor beside the bed. "So we can lie down."

"Why do you want to lie down."

"On the bed." He motioned toward it.

His wife lifted a pair of silk stockings from the drawer and bent over to set them in the suitcase.

"Lisa?"

"No, Bill."

He stepped to the window, pulled the curtain across it and looked back at his wife.

She shook her head.

Then he pulled the top blanket up across the unmade bed and smoothed it. He seated himself on the edge and reached down to untie a shoe.

"Are you going to bed?" she said, reaching into the drawer again.

"I want to make a bond between us."

"That's not the answer," she said, lifting out a sweater.

"Lisa."

"N-O," she said.

"Why is your mind set on going back up with your sister." He got up from the bed. "Do you know?"

"I do."

"Because I don't, and you aren't going till I do."

Lisa got down beside the suitcase and snapped its locks. Then she stood.

William reached over to take the handle.

"Are we going to have a tug-of-war now?"

"Give it to me."

"No."

He yanked it out of her hand, then stood holding it at his side.

Lisa walked past him to the window. She pushed back the curtain, then turned a small crank till the window opened. "I'm ready!" she called, putting a hand beside her mouth.

William walked over to the window and cranked it closed, glancing down at Nan, who was floating on her back just past the breaker line. "She didn't hear you."

"I'll tell you why I'm going back with her," Lisa said. "I think I can find a better life for myself than I've found with you. Does that answer your question?"

"No."

"Do you really want to know what I think of you," she said, taking a step toward him. "Do you?"

"All right."

"Do you or not want to know what I think of you, William."

"I'd like to he said. "Realizing your ideas right now are the ones Nan's put in your head."

"I'm not brainwashed."

William nodded.

"The only person who ever tried to brainwash me was you," she said, "and I'm telling you now you didn't succeed."

"Let's lie down." He seated himself on the edge of the bed again. "Really. You're starting to get aggressive."

"Be meek," she said.

"Don't be meek; just lower your voice."

"I'm going to tell you something about yourself."

William looked up at her a few moments, then bent over and tied his shoe. "I'm doing all right, Lisa."

"You're afraid of me, aren't you."

"No."

"You're scared stiff of me."

He got up and walked around the bed. "I'll carry your suitcase down."

"Aren't you."

"No, Lisa."

"You're afraid to hear why I'm leaving you, aren't you."

"You don't know why, Lisa." He picked up the suitcase. "Go back to San Marino, think things over, have some more conversations with Nan if you're enjoying them. You'll land on your feet by and by." He carried the suitcase out the door and started down the stairs.

"I'm married to a fairy," she said.

William stopped. For a few moments it was quiet, then Lisa appeared on the top stair. "Did you hear me?"

"I'll say just one thing," he said, "then I don't want this to come up again. It's fun for you to have your drama, to play people off against each other. This adds zest to your routine." He cleared his throat. "But you have a decision."

Lisa crossed her arms over her chest and leaned against the wall. "You're a fairy."

"You're a mature person, in years, if not in other ways, and you . . ."

"Did you hear me?"

"I heard you," he said. "Your sister likes throwing names around. You can look at her and Chester and see there's something wrong. But . . ."

"You wanted to know why I'm leaving," she said, "and now I'm telling you: you're a fairy."

William looked at one of the steps a moment, then started back up. "Here," he said, holding out the suitcase. "Put these back—you're not going anywhere."

"You don't like to hear that, do you."

"No."

"But that's what you are."

"Put your clothes away," he said. "You and Nan have seen enough of each other."

Suddenly she raised her leg up and kicked the end of the suitcase, knocking it out of his hand. It fell against the wall, then rolled part way down the stairs before stopping.

"I'll thank Nan for bringing you down here."

"When I saw you sneaking down to spy on those girls the other night, that's when I first started to realize I was married to a fairy."

William came up one step. "Don't say that again."

"Don't call you a a fairy?"

"No."

She smiled. "It bothers you, doesn't it."

"It bothers me," he said, "because you can do better."

"The sex magazines," she said. "All the things you do are fairyish—not that you can help it. I realize it's the way you are."

William took another step up the stairs. "I married you because I loved you."

"Oh that's nice."

"It's hard to say under the circumstances," he said, staring up at her, "but I've loved you always. I love you now."

"How can fairies love women," she said. "I thought they only loved other men."

Suddenly William brought his hand back and then slammed it against his wife's face. She fell against the wall but then recovered.

"It gives you pleasure to hurt women, doesn't it."

"Not to hurt you, Lisa."

She looked down at the suitcase.

"Has this last year and a half really been so horrible?"

"Yes."

"No, it hasn't."

She nodded.

"Maybe it has," he said, "but we're going to make it better."

"Why don't you hit me some more," she said. "You're more sincere when you do that." She started down the stairs, but he put his hand against the wall to stop her. "Please let me by."

"Think what's wrong with the marriage, Lisa. Specifically. What I'm doing wrong, and we'll make changes. *I'll* make changes."

She rested her hand on his arm. "I'm not trying to be mean when I say this," she said. "I know Nan's a bitch; I'm not trying to be like her." She turned to look at him. "But you just . . . really, you can't change, so it's pointless to say it to you, and it's mean, but you aren't enough of a person in certain ways. Excuse me." She ducked under his arm and walked down, picking up her suitcase from the stairs.

"Sex?" William said.

She carried the suitcase on down to the bottom.

William went down after her. "Sex?" he said. "Are you talking about that?"

She walked out the door of the living room.

"Are you?" he said, following her. "Lisa?"

"I'm talking about everything." She walked out onto the small grassy area in front of the house and up to the low wall, where she set down the suitcase.

William walked up behind her. "We've never talked about sex point blank," he said, "have we."

She shook her head.

"We've alluded to it," he said, "but we've never actually got it out in the open and kicked it around." He stepped up beside her. "Shall we?"

"If you have to talk about it," she said, "what's the point."

"Sometimes it's good," he said, "and other times it's a little slow, I'll admit. But I'd say it was good more than slow."

Lisa folded her arms across her chest and looked out toward the horizon.

"Let me tell you one thing," William said. "One lunch hour I was at the newsstand next to the office and got one of those manuals—the sex manuals; positions from different countries: Thailand, some of those. Then I took it back to the office and looked through it during the afternoon. But it didn't seem relevant. It just said you shouldn't be ashamed of thinking up new ways of doing it. Shall we talk about this?" He looked down at a large cactus plant growing up from the other side of the wall. "Maybe it's something people should bring out and discuss with each other: different positions, manner of insertion. . . ."

"Look," she said, turning toward him, "just till Nan comes up do you think I could stand here and enjoy the air, the sea."

"You don't want to . . ."

"I don't want to talk about manner of insertion, no." She looked back out at the ocean.

"But you said I didn't measure up, Lisa."

She reached down for the suitcase.

"You said that."

"I know," she said, "and now you'll nag and needle me for an hour about it."

"I won't."

"You've started."

"I haven't."

She looked back out over the ocean. "Now the intimidation starts," she said. "I mean I don't even have to listen to your words any more. Just the tone of your voice. The intimidating will go on for a few minutes, then turn to self-pity, or something else."

William seated himself on the wall. "Am I intimidating you?" he said softly.

Lisa glanced at her watch. "We'll see how long the intimidating lasts today."

"You didn't answer me," he said very quietly. "Am I intimidating you?"

"Yes."

"I am?"

She nodded.

"How, Lisa."

"I don't know," she said, "just your manner."

"I'm not intimidating you," he said.

"You may be trying not to," she said, "but you can't help it."

"You're wrong, Lisa."

"I'm not wrong."

"You *are* wrong!" he said, getting up. "You tell me

I'm intimidating you, but you don't tell me how. You tell me I don't measure up, but you don't explain what you mean. You call me a fairy. Lisa?"

"Yes, William."

"What the hell."

She looked out at the ocean again.

"Really," he said. "Let's hear it straight."

The wind ruffled through her hair.

"I don't understand," he said.

"You don't understand why it's annoying to have someone standing beside you jabbering while you look out over the ocean?" she said. "You don't understand that?"

"But if it wasn't for me," he said, "you wouldn't even be at the ocean."

She nodded. "That's about it."

"What is."

"If it wasn't for you," she said. "Every minute of every day I'm reminded that everything I wear, use and touch is paid for by you."

"It is—so what."

She took a deep breath.

"Do I make a fuss over money? No. If you need money, I give it to you. How did money get into this."

"I feel guilty every time I spend a penny of your money—that's all I know."

"Maybe you feel guilty because you aren't spending it wisely."

"I see."

"Money," he said. "Do you really think that's relevant to this?"

"No."

He took her suitcase and set it on the grass. "You're suggesting I begrudge my money too much."

"No, Bill."

"Would you be happier if you had more money?" He reached into his back pocket for his wallet, removed two twenty-dollar bills and held them out. "Take these."

"What for."

"Take them." He shook them in front of her. "Really. Go shopping."

She took them from him and William returned the wallet to his pocket. "What do you need," he said.

"I might get a skirt."

"Fine." He turned slightly so he could look out over the sea. "When shall we go to the store," he said. "After we've said goodbye to Nan?"

She held out the bills. "Here."

"What for."

"Take them."

"You don't want to shop?"

"I thought maybe Nan and I could go to a shop in San Marino, after my appointment."

He looked down at the bills for a few moments, then took them back.

"There's strings attached to everything you do for me," she said, "isn't there."

"No." He removed the wallet again and returned the money to it. "But I am the one who works for it."

Lisa reached up and waved. William looked down at Nan, floating on her back just outside the breaker line. She waved back and called.

"I can't hear you!" Lisa called back.

Nan cupped her hands beside her mouth. "Did you want to start back?"

A wave splashed up onto the sand.

"Whenever you're ready!"

Nan jumped up in the water, then splashed back down. "The water's marvelous!"

"Lisa," William said, "we seem to be communicating a little better than when you first came. . . ."

"Who is."

"*We* are," he said. "Tell her you're staying down here so we can talk over our problems."

"You think we're communicating better than when I first came down here."

"Don't you?"

"No."

"You don't think we feel more natural with each other."

"No."

"That's funny," he said. "I thought we did."

They watched as Nan swam on her back out toward the buoy.

"I'll tell you what I hope you'll do," Lisa said, turning toward him. "Finish your vacation, try and get rested, then go back up and start work again. When you feel like it call up and we'll arrange conferences." She picked up her suitcase.

"You mean conferences with us and the counselor."

"Yes."

William nodded. "Well I'm sure we don't need any counselor, Lisa."

She turned and walked across the grass.

"Why do we need a counselor," he said.

"Because we do." She started down the steps leading to the sand below. "We can't solve our problems by ourselves."

"We can."

"But we haven't," she said. "We haven't even talked about them."

He started down after her, keeping one step behind on the narrow concrete stairs. "We'll start now."

"We don't know how."

"Look," he said, "why are you carrying your suitcase to the beach."

"I want to keep it with me."

"May I carry it?"

"I have it."

William glanced down at two boys lying on their towels, looking up at them through sun glasses.

"Nan brought up the counselor, didn't she."

"Yes."

"Well let's find one down here," he said. "If you're set on it, let's look in the phone book for one here at the beach."

She got to the bottom and stepped down onto the sand.

"You look idiotic walking around down here with a suitcase, Lisa."

"Don't stay with me."

He walked beside her toward the water. "Set your suitcase on the steps. Really. It looks odd."

She went down to the damp part of the sand, set the suitcase on its end and seated herself on it.

"Why be weird."

She waved at her sister, who was holding onto the buoy out past the breakers.

"Let's get down to cases here, Lisa."

Nan waved back.

"Lisa?"

"I'm listening," she said. She reached down and pulled off her shoes, then got up, picked up the suitcase and began walking along the damp sand. William stepped back as a wave splashed up over his wife's feet and toward his own shoes, then walked beside her. Lisa stepped over a partially washed-away sand castle. They walked without speaking down toward the end of the cove. Two children with red shovels ran past them and into a wave.

"Shall I tell you something Nan told me?" Lisa said.

"What was it."

"I'll tell you some other time." She dug the toes of one of her feet into the sand as she walked and kicked some wet sand up ahead of her.

"What was it," he said.

"Just what someone said to her."

"About what."

She kicked some more sand ahead of her. "About you," she said. "It was someone who used to know you."

"When."

"When you were younger."

They neared the cliff at the end of the cove. Lisa set her suitcase on its end again and sat down.

"What is it," William said. "A bad thing?"

Lisa shrugged.

"I'd like to know."

"It might just be a rumor," she said. "I wouldn't want to spread it any farther if it was."

"Let me set it to rest."

"A person in a group Nan belongs to said it. A group of ladies who help the poor. This person went to grammar school with you."

"Who was it."

Lisa looked out at some girls jumping and laughing in the surf. "This group of ladies was helping the poor one day, having a rummage sale in someone's garage, and Nan mentioned you were her brother-in-law. The other lady said you'd both been in the same class together in grammar school and told Nan something you'd done."

William looked down at the sand. "What," he said. A wave washed up across the sand toward their feet but then sunk down before it got to them. "That was of course some time ago," William said.

"I know."

"Did she say what grade it was?"

"Fourth."

William nodded. "That would make it some twenty years ago," he said. "It must have been a hot piece of gossip to have lasted down that long."

"Shocking."

"Can you say what it was?"

Lisa reached down to make a line in the wet sand with her finger.

"I think I know what it was," he said, "if it happened in fourth."

"What was it."

A wave washed up around William's shoes and around the base of the suitcase. Lisa picked it up and moved back to a dry place. She sat down on the sand and brushed a piece of brown seaweed off the bottom of the suitcase.

"Tell me this much," William said, sitting down beside her, "did it happen with five other people."

"It happened with some others."

"That's what I thought." He looked down at a dry brown seaweed bulb by one of his feet, then picked it up and popped it. "It's humorous in retrospect. It wasn't funny at the time." He tossed the bulb up and caught it, then turned to look at his wife. "I can't help but wonder how accurately the telling of the incident has come down through the years."

Lisa shrugged.

"Tell me how you got it from Nan and I'll tell you if that's how it happened."

She turned to look at him. "Did you really do that?"

"I don't know."

She laughed.

"It's probably been exaggerated. Who was the friend of Nan's who was in my class. Was her name Faith Thompson?"

"No."

"Faith was the one who spread it around the school originally."

"Clara something."

William nodded. "Clara Rivers."

"That was it."

"I'll tell you something about Clara Rivers, just to set the record straight. A few days after it happened, after the principal had called all our parents and told them about it, after we'd all been sent home for a week, Clara Rivers called me up and asked if she could do it with us the next time. Tell Nan that part of it before the next rummage sale."

"I will."

"Clara Rivers," William said. He looked down at the sand for a while. "So she still wishes she'd been invited." He set down the broken seaweed bulb. "Maybe we ought to have a twentieth reunion of the original five and include her this time." He got up and brushed off the back of his pants. "Lisa, why are we sitting here talking about a time when I was nine years old when the janitor caught us in the cloakroom with our pants down, playing dirty choo-choo train during recess from Miss Falvey's class." He brushed off the back of his pants again. "What's happening."

Lisa got up and picked up her suitcase.

"Let's get some perspective, Lisa."

"I'd like to."

He glanced down at Nan out by the buoy. "But we won't get it by you going up to San Marino and hearing dirty stories from grammar school."

"Can I ask how you play dirty choo-choo train?"

"We'll get perspective here," he said, "by talking things out."

Lisa started slowly back toward the other end of the cove. "I get perspective by thinking things over," she said.

"With an atmosphere like Chester and Nan's house? Wise up, Lisa."

A man walked in front of them toward the ocean, adjusting a green face mask over his chin.

"Lisa . . ."

"You see," she said, "you're pressing me. You're always pressing me. But I finally realized I don't have to sit by and let you do it any more."

William stopped in front of her. "No more pressing," he said.

"Have you ever seen Chester pressing Nan?"

"No, and I'll tell you why."

"You don't have to." She walked around him.

He moved in front of her again. "I'll ask you just one question," he said. "Do you want to be like Nan. Do you want that kind of life."

"I want to be free like she is."

"Her? Free?"

"She doesn't let anyone push her around like I do." She stepped around him again. "Like I used to."

He walked beside her. "Look . . ."

"You look," she said, stopping and turning toward him. "Every time there's a problem, every time anything comes up, you press me till I give in. But not this time, Bill." She pointed at his face. "Because I finally did wise up." She looked at him a moment longer, then lowered her arm and started on along the sand.

"But Nan . . ."

"I know what you think of Nan," she said, "but what can you offer better."

"Just ourselves, Lisa."

"No."

"Right from the first," he said, "I thought the point was we didn't need a lot of friends—that social kind of life."

"Then why are we so bored down here that we can't even look at each other."

"I don't know."

"We're bored," she said, "because we stop each other from thinking. We sit around waiting for the other person to come up with an idea."

Nan was waving again from beyond the breakers. William glanced at her, noticed that Lisa hadn't seen her, then decided not to wave back. "Stagnation," he said. "Is that what you're saying?"

"Dry rot."

"Well let's overcome it."

A wave splashed over her feet. "We don't know how."

"Let's just start by starting," he said. "We'll start by thinking of something to do."

Lisa set down the suitcase again, seated herself and folded her arms across her chest. "Go ahead."

"Well it would have to be both of us thinking of it," he said.

She nodded. "Do you see what's happening?"

"But you've got to try too, Lisa."

She unfolded her arms and rested the palms of her hands on the corners of the suitcase. "I'll try then," she said. "I'm trying to think of something to do."

Several waves lapped up toward them, then fell back into the sea. "You see?" she said, looking up at him.

"You haven't tried."

"I tried as hard as I could to think of something I wanted to do with you." She shook her head. "Nothing."

William snapped his fingers. "We'll go up the coast," he said. "We'll stop along the way for some lunch, then during the afternoon we'll visit the marine aquarium."

Lisa made a circle in the sand with her big toe.

"Okay?"

"Bill, then there's tomorrow, and we already will have driven up the coast and had lunch along the way and seen the sea aquarium. And there's the day after that, and the day after that." She got up from her suitcase and took a step toward him. "You sit over in your office all day, Bill, and I sit home. As long as you're over there all day I can kid myself that I'll stop being so bored as soon as a vacation comes."

William nodded toward several men and women in bathing suits a few yards from where they were standing. "Some people are listening."

"I can sit there staring out the window over the washing machine thinking of the fun in the sun when Bill gets his three weeks," she said, her voice rising. "And when you come home sullen and hostile I can say it's because he's tired, he's worked hard making money so we can have fun, if we just wait awhile."

"Lisa."

"And on the weekends," she said, "the boring, horrible weekends!"

He noticed that she had started to cry.

"Sitting around pools with prematurely fat bankers and stockbrokers with drinks in their floating styrofoam drink holders, I can pretend it's going to be worth it—someday something will happen to make it all worth it."

William glanced at the group sitting on their towels, then reached over to take his wife's arm, but she pulled away.

"But it won't, Bill," she said. "It won't change! Nothing will change! Do you see?"

William turned to see Nan striding up out of the surf. "Here comes your sister."

"It won't change," she said, wiping her cheek with the back of her hand, "unless I make it change. I've come to see that." She wiped her other cheek. "I'm truly sorry to embarrass you by making a scene in front of the other people on the beach. But at this moment embarrassment is the only and the most profound emotion that I feel for you."

"Golly what water!" Nan said, coming up beside them, throwing droplets off one of her arms. She glanced at Lisa, then at William. "I don't see how you can stay out a minute." She pushed her wet hair back over her head. "Do you have the time, Bill?"

He looked at his watch. "Almost one."

"Are you ready, Lisa?"

"Yes."

Nan started toward the towel. "I can't thank you enough for the swim, Bill. I don't know how I would have gotten through the week up there without it." She bent over, picked up the towel and dried off her face. Then she looked down at the top part of her bathing suit. "Oh dear." She reached down and pulled the material out from her chest. "Is this material starting to tear?"

William looked down into the top of the bathing suit at one of her breasts.

Nan looked up at him. "Oh." She pushed the top of the suit back flat against herself.

"I wasn't . . ."

"I'll be in the car," Lisa said. She started up the stairs.

"Shouldn't you help Lisa with that heavy bag?"

William turned around and started up the stairs after his wife. "Please let me help you," he said.

The storm started somewhere off the coast of Baja California, then began moving northward. As it moved it stayed right on the coast, some of the rain falling into the ocean and some falling on the beaches and up over the highway. The people who were at the beach, renting a house for the month or staying overnight in a motel or cottage, felt sure, since it was August in Southern California, that the storm would be an extremely short one, and, as planned, they carried their towels, umbrellas and plastic inner tubes out of their houses and apartments and motels and onto the sand.

But as it turned out the storm wasn't a short one, because as it moved slowly up along the coast it also stayed where it had been before and enlarged in a long oblong gray shape, starting down a few miles out from Guadalajara, in Mexico, and stretching up a few miles past Santa Barbara, sometimes thinning here and there. Sometimes people would come out from under their beach umbrellas, rub their hands together and say to the others around them that it was passing. But it didn't. It hung over the sea and the land in a gray mass, and in some places the dark cloud only went up to the other side of the highway so that the people on the beach could turn around and point up over the cliff at the blue sky and sunlight they saw there, even while it rained on them. But it continued to cling to the sandy beaches and over the water, at least as far out as anyone would want to swim.

In the northern part of Laguna Beach the people thought perhaps it wouldn't come as far up as they were. One beach was especially crowded and a man on it, wearing a red bathing suit, got up from his towel when he saw the dark clouds approaching and began pushing his arms through the air as though to push them back from where they'd come. Several other people were lying on towels beside him, and they all laughed as they watched him. However, it had no effect on the progress of the storm and a few minutes later the man who had been pushing at the clouds was wrapping himself in two large beach towels and moving up against the cliff.

Above these people, in the kitchen of his rented beach house, William Alren was sitting at a breakfast table, as he had been for over an hour since his wife had left, looking at a toaster.

His first awareness of the storm was a plinking sound

just outside the door. He turned his head. A drop had fallen into a pail. He watched a second drop hit a flagstone, then turned his head back to look at the toaster again and listened as the drops began falling faster, occasionally plinking into the bucket but usually splattering onto the flagstones. When he looked out again they had turned to a splotchy brown.

William got up and walked slowly into the living room to the large bay window. He looked down at the beach. Most of the people had left the sand, although there were three umbrellas up at different places, people still under them, and several people were in the water, riding in the waves, even though it was raining on them. William looked down at the gray ocean for a while, then up at the gray sky, then finally walked across the room and upstairs. He removed a bathing suit from one of the bureau drawers and carried it to the bed. He seated himself, bent over and untied a shoe. Then he unbuckled his belt and began removing his pants. But just as he was pulling them down there was a bright flash of lightning out the window. He looked out a moment at the sky, then pulled his pants back up and bent over and tied his shoe again. He sat on the bed, the bathing suit resting on one knee, and listened to the rain as it fell onto the roof. While he sat there he decided to take a walk. Then, when the rain ceased falling so hard, he went downstairs and to a closet in the living room, where he had seen an umbrella a few days before. He got it out, carried it outside and opened it, then started slowly up the driveway to the street.

First he walked along the street and by the cliff where he'd gone with Nan, then he walked past some wet stucco apartment houses and past another beach. For a few minutes it stopped raining altogether and he closed the umbrella and carried it at his side, but then it started again and he opened it and put it over his head. After the first beach the street went up and along past some wet palm trees. Out over the ocean, just at the horizon, was a thin line of blue sky. He watched it as he walked, and as he watched it slowly was closed over by the gray and disappeared.

At one place William stopped and looked at an old man wearing a plastic raincoat as he stood and rolled a small black bowling ball across a green lawn. He rolled several more. When he had rolled the last one he walked down to the other end, gathered them up and rolled them back to where he had been before. William looked down past more palm trees and past a bed of wet orange flowers. He decided not to walk any farther. He opened the umbrella over his head and turned around to start back and it was just then that he saw the girl.

She had no shoes on and was wearing a short skirt and a blue denim shirt with its two flaps tied in front of her in a knot. Even though she was all the way across the street William could tell the moment she turned the corner that she had no bra on.

She walked down the sidewalk past several houses, then turned and walked up a path leading to a house. He watched her go up some wooden steps, past a sign and in through the front door.

William closed his umbrella. He walked slowly down the sidewalk till he was just opposite the house, then he stepped off the walk and beside a palm tree. In through the glass of the front door he could see the girl wringing out her hair. He watched her open another door and step through it. Then, because the room was in the front of the house, he watched as she entered it. A moment later she came to the windows and pushed them open. She glanced across the street at William. He looked quickly off at a parked car. When he looked back she was still standing there, her hand resting on the glass of the window, looking out at him. She didn't smile, but stood with her wet hair in a thick rope falling down beside her shoulder. Again William looked away, this time up at a heavy gray cloud overhead. He waited, then looked back again. She was still standing as she had been before, looking directly across the street and at his eyes. A white car passed between their line of vision. When it was gone she nodded at him twice, slowly, then moved back away from the window. Just before she got back to where it was too dark to see her she put her hands up under her breasts and squeezed them.

William walked quickly around to the other side of the palm tree. He stared at a dry place on its bark. He looked around the edge of it. The windows were still open, but the girl wasn't in sight. Quickly he twisted the gold band off the third finger of his left hand. He took his wallet out of his back pocket and pushed the ring down into it between some bills. When the wallet was back in his pocket he gripped the handle of the umbrella tightly and stepped back around the palm tree and onto the sidewalk.

Two cars passed, then William stepped onto the street and walked across it and up onto the other side. He walked up the path leading between two rows of white stones and up the stairs, glancing at a sign at the top, which said "No Vacancy." He pushed open the front door and went inside.

There was a door on one side with the numeral "1" on it, then a flight of wooden stairs. Another door at the base of the stairs had a bronze "2" on it. It was an inch or two open. William stood a moment at the foot of the stairs, then stepped over toward it. Looking through the crack he could see the side of an icebox. He jumped slightly as a door opened and closed upstairs, but there was no more sound except the rain, which had begun suddenly to fall more heavily. Slowly, William reached out with the end of his umbrella and touched the door. He pushed it. It opened another inch. He pushed again and it opened enough so that he could see the girl, standing on the other side of the room.

William stepped up to the door, then through it. He closed it behind him.

The girl was standing in front of a cupboard, looking up into it, her back to William. She continued standing there even after he'd come in. Then, without turning around to look at him, she reached up and brought down a pan. She carried it to a sink and filled it with water. William opened his mouth to say something. Instead of saying it, though, he closed it again and watched as the girl rested the pan on the burner of a stove in the corner and twisted a knob beneath it. Then she stepped back and turned around toward William. "Can you put down your umbrella?" she said.

William rested the handle of his umbrella, which was a red and white plaid one, against the door. It fell to the floor. He bent over and picked it up, made sure it was resting securely, then looked back at the girl. She raised one of her hands to a breast. William watched her move the hand up toward her neck, then hook her thumb in the neck of her wet shirt. They stood quietly across the room from each other, not moving, till finally the girl turned and walked to a low bed against the wall. Keeping her eyes on William she seated herself. She pulled her skirt up over her hips and William saw she had nothing on beneath the skirt. She continued looking at him, then lay down on her back, resting one of her hands on the inner part of her leg and placing one foot on the floor beside the bed.

William looked over at the window and at some palm trees, then back at the girl in the dim gray light. She kept her head turned toward the wall, her eyes closed. William turned toward the door. There was a latch on it. He slid it quietly into place. Water was running down across his face from his hair. He brushed some out of his eyes, then took two steps across the room and stopped. Her legs open, one of her feet on the floor, the girl let her lips part slightly. William reached down for his belt and unbuckled it. He unfastened the clasp of the pants and brought them down around his hips, then stood holding them and looking at the girl. Her lips parted more. William took several steps over toward the bed. The girl lay on the green corduroy spread, her narrow fingers resting against her leg. Finally he kneeled on the bed between her legs and moved down on top of her. She opened her mouth wider and sucked in her breath. William's cheek pressed against hers; with one hand he continued holding his belt buckle and the material of his pants so they wouldn't go farther down than his knees. He felt a soft, hot breast flattening up against his chest. The girl reached down between them with her long fingers and took hold of him.

They lay quietly, William staring at the worn bedspread and at a place on it an inch or two from his eye where water had dropped down from his hair. The girl lay beneath him. They had moved up toward the top part of the bed so that William's forehead was off the end of it. It was still raining, but not as hard, then there was the sound of boiling water. The girl moved. "The water," she said.

"Oh."

She moved out from under him, William raising himself while she slid out. Then she walked over to the corner, pushing her skirt down around her legs again. William turned on his side, holding the pants at the level of his knees, and watched as she reached up into the cupboard for a cup and a container of chocolate powder. She shook some of the powder into the cup and carried it to the stove, where she poured the water in on the powder. William turned on his stomach. He pulled the pants back up, then buckled them and zipped them, balancing himself on his toes and his forehead as he did. He ran his fingers through his hair and sat up on the bed. After smoothing one of his pants legs he looked over at the girl: she was sitting at a table drinking her hot chocolate. She took a sip and glanced up at a window overhead. William turned his face down toward the floor and sat awhile looking at the floorboards. Finally he looked back at the girl.

She sat with her elbows on the table, the rim of the cup against her lower lip.

William cleared his throat. "I don't know exactly what to say."

She didn't turn her head.

Slowly William got to his feet. "Are you . . ." He took a step toward her.

"Am I what," she said.

"Are you renting this place?"

She lowered the cup down to the table.

"This apartment," he said, motioning toward one of the walls. "This room. Are you renting it."

She turned her face to look at him. "Yes."

He nodded toward a bookcase against the wall. "Good," he said, "it's . . . I like it. We're renting a house on down the way." He pointed in the direction of his house. "Down about half a mile or so. Are you having . . . is this a vacation for you?"

She watched him without answering.

"This," William said, smiling. "A vacation is it? For you?"

She nodded.

"Yes," he said, "well it's too bad about the rain, although I don't think it will last." He glanced out the window at the rain. "Are you . . . do you work?" He made a circular motion with his arm. "Is this a vacation you're taking from your job?"

"Yes, it is."

"Very good." William made a clicking sound with his lips. "Near here?"

"In La Habra."

"Ah," he said, "yes."

She took another sip of the hot chocolate and then turned and looked at the wall.

"Your work," William said, "I was just wondering. . . ."

"I'm in a secretarial pool."

"Oh yes." William made another clicking sound with his mouth, then looked down at one of his hands. "Well then." There was a silence. "Oh say, you don't have the time by any chance."

She looked at the watch on his wrist.

"Oh, right. Forgot I had it on." He looked down at it.

"Gee, I have to go," he said, looking up at her.

"Goodbye."

"I have some friends I have to go see. I have to get started."

"Goodbye."

William turned around and walked to the door for his umbrella. "Well," he said, picking it up, "this is a good spot for a vacation." He unlocked the door. "I know this weather won't hold on," he said, opening the door. "I wouldn't worry." He stepped part way through it and looked back at the girl. "Well," he said, smiling and raising his hand. "Adios." He watched her raise the cup slowly toward her lips, then stepped out into the hallway and closed the door.

He walked quickly out the door, down the steps and to the sidewalk, then started talking to himself. "Crazy," he said. "Completely crazy. You'd think she'd have offered me some cocoa."

A man leading a dog on a leash walked toward him.

"I've got to think," William said.

The man stopped. "What?"

"Nothing." He hurried on. *What difference does it make what happened; it must make some. A reason for it? She was beautiful—why is she going to bed with someone off the sidewalk. If she'd been more friendly I would have stayed. If she'd wanted to get some problem off her chest I would have listened even without going to bed. I could go back.* He stopped a moment at a curb. *I could spend the night with her, talk.* He turned around and started very slowly back the way he had come. *I'll say something this time: "What is it, what's wrong? I don't understand. May I help in some way." Does she want me to come back?* He stopped. *"I'm sorry about before. I was mechanical before. Forgive me for not speaking, being automatic." Will she cry if I go back? I'll put my arms around her. "What is it, tell me, What can I do." I said adios to her. "I'm sorry I was insincere when I left. But I'm a married person; I should have told you; I took my ring off behind the palm tree. You see, my wife's left me; I'm confused. Right now I'm going through a troubled period. If we could help each other somehow. By talking? Let's go up to the highway and have a snack." Why did I say adios? I've never said it before—only in Spanish class. "Look, whatever your name is, I didn't know how to act before; that's why I said adios." It's raining harder; I'm catching cold, a sore throat. What if she had syphilis.* He looked down at rain falling onto a wet square of concrete in front of him. *I should have washed myself. What do they say: always wash with hot soapy water within five minutes afterwards? Ten minutes? Penicillin. Do they have to ream you out? They don't do that any more—not with modern medicine. The signs: sores on the neck two weeks afterwards? Bleeding lips? Brain deterioration. I could go to a gas station and wash myself. Cold water. I'll go back, wash in her bathroom, talk. A cup of hot chocolate—I'll ask if I can have one with her (she wanted to offer me one but didn't know how). I was awkward. Not suave. Is she laughing at me? I didn't satisfy her. My head aches.* He put his hands up against the sides of his head. *Pregnant? She must take pills—anyone as suave as she was. Could it be her first time? No. How old. Twenty-four, -five. She knew what she was doing. I just walked in the door, pulled my pants down and did it on the bed without anything else happening—no one seducing the other, not buying dinner for her or getting drunk. I'd like to tell someone about it. An incredible experience. Worth it, even though I'm unfaithful, even though I have clap. It's raining harder. I'll have pneumonia on top of syphilis. A decision: either I go back to my house or to a gas station and wash myself with soap and water. Or back to the girl. Who would believe this happened. Fifteen minutes? Not even that. In and out: and I could go back, do it again—walk in, lower my pants again and do it all over. Why don't I. Perfectly free—it might even be better the second time; know each other better. Just in and do it. The rain outside. Romantic. Like something you hope for, for years: a fantasy. And it could happen again. Within three minutes I could be doing it again; I feel ready to go again. For free. It's raining down my neck but I'm going back.* Again he began walking toward her house, slowly at first, then faster. *Again. And then again. I'll spend the night with her. We'll talk: her problems, my problems. We'll talk all night, kissing, in the narrow bed, making love, beautifully, endlessly.* When he got back to the house he turned in the walk, then hurried up the steps, taking two at a time. He pushed through the front door. He stepped up to the girl's door, stood a moment catching his breath, then knocked. "Oh no," he said, withdrawing his hand.

The sound of the girl walking across the room. William took a step backward as the door opened.

"Yes?" the girl said.

"It was my wallet," he said, backing into a small table in the hallway. "I thought I'd left it." He reached into his back pocket, removed it and held it up. "But I have it. Thank you. Sorry." He turned, pushed back out the door and ran down the steps, slipping on the wet walk but catching his balance. He turned and hurried toward his house, clutching the wallet. *Don't dwell on what she thinks of you.* He began running along the sidewalk. *I could still go back for ten minutes, tell her I'm married. There's no possibility of doing it again with her, but if she has a problem I'll hear it and offer advice. Best to forget her. But you can't just sleep with someone, then go home (or can you). Pay her? Give her twenty dollars, thank her and then go home. Forget her. She got some free sex and a memory to take back to the secretarial pool. She may be pregnant. I may have gonorrhea. Even steven.* William stopped, opened his wallet and reached inside for the wedding ring. He pushed it back onto his finger, and returned the wallet to his pocket. *Lisa?* He started running again through the rain toward his house. *Lisa?* He started running faster.

Part Two

FOUR

At the end of the afternoon William drove up beside the curb, stopped, got out of his car and walked over a dichondra lawn to Nan and Chester's front porch. He rang the doorbell and listened to chimes sounding inside. In a few seconds a small wooden panel in the center of the door was pulled back and the upper part of Nan's face appeared on the other side. "Oh," she said. She looked at him a moment.

"May I come in please."

She closed the panel. After a few more instants the door opened.

"I'd like to see Lisa."

"Well she's busy."

"I need to see her."

Nan stood holding the doorknob. "Has something happened?"

"Yes, I've come to see her."

In the hallway behind Nan a young boy appeared wearing pajamas. "Who is it," the boy said.

"Uncle Bill."

"I want to see Lisa now."

The boy looked at William, then walked back down the hallway.

Nan stepped out onto the porch. "Mark's getting over the flu."

"You can just tell her I'm here," William said, "if you don't want me in the house."

Nan glanced down the street. "Chester should be home soon," she said. She looked at her watch.

"Lisa!" William called into the house.

Nan reached behind her and closed the front door. "Bill, she's resting right now. Don't imply I don't want you in the house—that's ridiculous. But I don't think this would be a good time to disturb her. She's resting and thinking." She put her hands into the pockets of an apron she was wearing.

"How long will she be doing that."

Nan stepped down off the porch and seated herself on the step. "Let's just sit down here a minute."

William looked down at the brick step a moment, then sat down.

"First of all," Nan said, placing her hands on her knees, "let me say that neither Chester or I could ever have any bad feelings about you personally, no matter what happens in all this. Please understand that, Bill."

"I'll try."

"Never, Bill. We know the tremendous pressures you're under at this time and we respect you for it."

William glanced at the door. "I appreciate that," he said, getting up again. "Right now I'd like to go see Lisa."

Nan got up quickly and opened the door. She reached around and turned something on the other side, then pulled it closed again. She tried the knob and pushed at it but it didn't open. "Because we do understand you," she said, "and what you're going through at this time, we want very badly to help you." She returned to her seat on the step.

"Nan."

"I want you to wait till Chester gets home before seeing Lisa," she said.

"Why."

"I'd feel better. I'd feel calmer about it if he was here." She patted the bricks beside where she was sitting. "Sit down again, Bill."

"I'll stand."

She looked out over the lawn for a few moments, then twisted her head and looked up at him. "Just this morning you were having a nice vacation; now you're here, without even calling. Is there an emergency?"

"Would you like me to go back to the beach and call first."

Nan looked out at her mailbox, resting atop its white post, beside the street. "Don't bring sarcasm into this," she said. "It's peaceful here. I'm calm. Lisa's calm. She's thinking things over. Can't you understand why I don't want you to go in there?"

"Yes."

"She says you don't allow her any peace. That's one of her . . ."

"All right."

"Do you see?"

"I see."

They waited, William standing on the step, Nan seated beside his shoe. William watched two birds fly down and land on the dichondra, hop around, then fly off. A car turned the corner. "Chester's car is like that," Nan said. "A little deeper blue." The car went slowly past, then turned into a driveway several houses down. "You don't smoke, do you, Bill."

"No."

"I wish I had your will power." She felt the pockets of her apron. "Promise me something," she said, getting up again. "If I let you into the house, promise you won't run in and see Lisa."

"I won't, Nan."

"Thank you." She lifted up a white ceramic dog at the side of the porch. Underneath it was a dead sow bug and the top of a key wedged into a crack between two bricks. She removed the key, opened the door with it, then returned it under the dog. "Go ahead."

William walked into the house.

Nan followed, closed the door, then walked past him into the living room and removed a cigarette from a dish on a low coffee table. She picked up a lighter from beside the dish. "Sit down, sit down." She gestured at the furniture.

William seated himself on a soft couch.

"A Coke, Bill?"

"No thank you."

"Not to keep harping away on the unpleasant side of this," she said, sitting down on a chair across from him, "but just let me say one thing: if it'll make you more relaxed I can tell you that help is on the way." She lit the cigarette and returned the lighter to the table.

"What help is this."

"Professional help." She took a deep drag from the cigarette. "Competent, qualified, professional help. In the form of a brilliant specialist named Dr. Sadler. Lisa had her first appointment with him this afternoon and she's completely crazy about him. You will be too. Let me get us two Cokes." She rose from her chair. "I'd rather have Chester explain how we found him," she said, pushing her hair back along the sides of her head as she left the room. "But he's a miracle, Bill. A walking, talking miracle of a man."

Over the fireplace was an oil painting of a café in France. William looked up at it. He listened as his sister-in-law opened and closed the door of the refrigerator in the kitchen, then as she uncapped the drinks and poured them, fizzing, into glasses. She returned, carrying two large glasses decorated with playing-card symbols, and held one out to William. "I didn't want a Coke," he said. He waited a moment, then took it.

When the honeymoon ended Nan and Chester invited the two of them over for dinner and to see their house. At that time they were staying with William's mother in Palos Verdes and looking for an apartment. About half way through the dinner party Nan began tapping her fork against her drinking glass, then when it was quiet she announced to the others, especially to William, smiling at him as she spoke, that she had found a house for the two of them, which was only eight blocks away, and which had a reasonable rent. If it wasn't within William's means, she announced that Chester would agree to help out at first till William got going at something.

William didn't say anything after the announcement, then when dinner was over they got into Chester's car and drove to the house, where a realtor was waiting to show them through. It was unfurnished, and they took nearly a half hour going through it and looking out at the back yard at some swings and a gardening shed. William followed the others while Nan talked about the sense of privacy they would have and how the floor plan allowed for a maximum freedom of movement from one room to the other, but without being far-out modernistic the way many of the new houses were. Then, on the way back to her and Chester's house, she began discussing the kind of curtains that would go best with the paneling in the den and it was at that time that William felt he should probably say something.

First he thanked her for thinking of them and said he liked the house and the neighborhood. Then he said they were thinking about an apartment, though, and would probably keep thinking of one, near, they hoped, to where William's mother lived, which was forty or fifty miles away. He explained that his father didn't live at home and that as long as he was in the area it would be good to be close to his mother.

Nan didn't talk the rest of the way home, but when the car stopped in the Morrises' driveway she said she'd already put down a month's rent for deposit and that it was non-refundable. William thanked her. He said he wasn't in a position to pay her back at that time but would when he could. Then they went inside the house again and William and Nan didn't speak the rest of the evening.

The apartment they finally took was in Pasadena, on a street called Los Robles, only several miles from Nan's and Chester's house. The first time Nan came over to see it, which was for dinner, she said it seemed quite small and that the house she'd found for them was still being held by her deposit and they could still move into it. William said he preferred the apartment. Then he said it seemed she should appreciate that they were living in Pasadena, rather than by his mother as they had planned, so that she and Lisa could see each other, and shop together, or whatever Nan had in mind. Nan said it was fun to have them close, but that he wasn't showing good sense to pass up the house she'd found for them. William said again that they'd taken the apartment specifically to have Lisa near enough to get together with Nan. At that point in the dinner Lisa was passing a rice and tuna dish. Her sister complimented her on it and didn't talk to William again.

"Tell me something," Nan said. She leaned forward and picked up her Coca-Cola. The coaster came part way up with it, then fell back down on the table. "Exactly what do you feel Lisa's role is."

William looked off into the dining room. There was a round table in the center of it with four wooden chairs placed around it. The wallpaper had a pattern of climbing ivy.

"Bill?"

He looked back at his sister-in-law.

"What do you think Lisa's role is in your marriage."

"I'm not sure."

"Then what do you think your role is."

"I'm not sure of that either."

"Because I think I know what you feel Lisa's role should be and what your role should be."

He continued looking at her over the table.

"I do, Bill."

"I'd like to hear."

Nan reached for the cigarette dish. "Bill," she said.

"Yes?"

"Don't play this game with me in my house."

"What game."

"Come on, Bill."

"I'm waiting for Chester so I can see Lisa. There's no game."

She lit the new cigarette, then stood and pointed at him, the cigarette between the two fingers she was pointing with. "You know what game I'm talking about, Bill."

He shook his head.

She reached up to remove something from her tongue. "You know, you don't *have* to see Lisa at all. Even after he comes there's no reason you have to see her."

William looked down at the table.

"You know that, don't you."

"I thought the idea . . ."

"The idea," Nan said, "is to get some of this secrecy out in the open, some of the things going around in your head. Because I know what they are." She stepped up to the mantelpiece. "You don't fool me, Bill."

"I'm not trying to."

She parted a wire-mesh screen in front of the fireplace and flicked her cigarette into it. "I realize it's part of your game to get me to spill first."

"Spill what."

"Oh, you're good at it," she said, straightening up again, "aren't you."

William reached for his Coke, sipped at it, then rested it on his knee.

"But I'll tell you something," she said. "You're going

to have to be a lot better. Because Lisa's here to stay till I say she can leave. And I have no intention of doing that till some of these ideas of yours are out in the open where she can deal with them." She took a drag from the cigarette and blew smoke up toward the ceiling. "I know the way you think, Bill," she said. "You think Lisa's role is the traditional role of the woman. Your role is the traditional role of the man."

William looked down at a strip of molding running along the base of the wall.

"Do you deny that?"

"No."

"You don't."

"No, I like to think of her as the woman, me as the man."

"Well you see that's where you go completely off into outer space, Bill." She pointed at him again, the cigarette still between her fingers. "That's where you're drawing on all the history of male repression of the female over the centuries and trying to force Lisa into that obsolete mold. The mold of the downtrodden, obedient and inferior sex, you see. Less endowed mentally. Able to produce and rear children, but not much else. Now in your case I don't think you're even conscious of this attitude, of the damage it's doing to both of you. But I'll be honest: I'm not sure if you're acting dumb so I'll let you go see Lisa when Chester comes, or if you're just a person who's not aware. But let's not mince words." She stepped out from the painted white bricks around the fireplace and onto the carpet, still pointing at him, smoke rising up from her hand. "You believe the male sex is superior to the female sex, don't you."

"No."

"In certain respects," Nan said, "you believe your sex is superior to mine, don't you." She seated herself suddenly beside him. "Don't take me for a fool, Bill."

"I don't."

"Because I'm not one. I promise you, if there's one thing I'm not, it's that."

"I don't think you are," he said, leaning forward to lift his drink up from the table again, "but I wonder if we couldn't just wait quietly till Chester comes."

"Put your Coke back."

His hand stopped where it was.

"Put it back on the table."

He returned it to its place.

"Now," she said, "stop the game too."

He continued looking at a piece of ice in his glass.

"Stop the game," she said, "because if you don't stop the game you won't see her, Chester or not. I promise you it's up to me whether or not you see her."

"Stop the game," he said.

"Now, William."

"I will."

"You will stop the game."

He nodded.

"Thank you," she said. "Now tell me the answer to my question."

"In certain respects," William said, "muscularly perhaps, men seem to have a superiority over women. Is that what you want me to say."

"Thank you, Bill." She got up again and returned to the fireplace. "We know where we stand now, don't we."

William glanced out the window as a car drove slowly past.

"Don't we."

"These kind of subjects never seem too fruitful to me."

"Then let me tell you something," she said, "and I think it's about time somebody did."

"Go ahead."

"I will," she said. "You're a smug, self-satisfied, conceited son-of-a-bitch, Bill."

He nodded.

"Stop nodding."

His head stopped.

"Did you hear what I said?"

"I heard," he said, "but I didn't come here to see you or fight with you."

"Well you are seeing me."

"I know."

"So you'd better stand up for yourself if you can."

"I have nothing to say to you."

She parted the wire curtain again and tossed the cigarette through it. "You'd better find something."

"This is your house," he said. "In a person's own house they can think and say what they want."

"Oh," she said, "and if I was at your house?"

"You'd be kicked out."

It was quiet while Nan ground out another cigarette in a glass ashtray on the table. "Let me tell you something, William Alren." She sat down across from him. "This may hurt just a little. I haven't spoken to anyone like this before except to my own husband. The only way I speak to you this way is because of my love for Lisa."

"I'll just make one comment first," he said. "It's obviously upsetting to you to have me sitting here on your couch. If you had something else to do till Chester came, fix your dinner or something. I'm sure it would be easier for both of us."

She reached for a new cigarette. "You're telling me to fix my dinner."

"I'm telling you it's unnecessary to fight."

She picked up the lighter and snapped at the top of it. "You feel so superior to me that all you have to say is 'Go fix the dinner, woman.' Isn't that it." She put the lighter back on the table without lighting her cigarette. Isn't it."

"This is absurd."

"And I'll tell you why it is."

"You don't have to."

"It's absurd," she said, "because I see through you, Bill Alren, like a plate of new glass, and you know it. Don't you."

"We're not connecting," he said, "because I didn't

come here for that reason. But let's be civil." He looked at her a moment, then picked up the lighter, snapped it till it was lit and held it toward the end of her cigarette.

"No thank you."

He returned it to the table.

"Shall I tell you why I don't want you to light my cigarette for me, chivalrous though the gesture may seem to you?"

"Nan."

"You don't lose your cool, do you, Bill." She returned the unlit cigarette to the cigarette box. "You don't ever lose your cool, do you."

"I do."

"But not very often."

"No."

"Do you treat Lisa like this?" Nan said.

"Lisa does not attack me with this degree of . . ."

She pointed at him. "Bill."

"Nan, you're making me sit here and wait till Chester comes home. You're insulting me. It seems plain to me you're either trying to drive me away or put on enough pressure till you get an emotional reaction from me. I'm not sure what an emotional reaction would gain for you, except I'd then have to apologize."

She looked at him across the table.

"I'll be as honest as I can," he said. "I don't understand how you think. At all."

"I've talked to you the way I sometimes talk to my own husband when he's needed some straightening out, Bill," she said, "but I don't think I'd better any more." She took a drag from a cigarette. "Chester's a man, thank God. And you're not, Bill. Let's pray it's not too late for you to grow up, but at this moment you have one awfully long way to go to manhood. Excuse me please." She got up, turned and walked quickly out of the room.

For a long time it was perfectly quiet in the house. William continued sitting on the couch, looking down at the table in front of him. Mark said something to himself in his room, then it was silent again. Outside the living room window was a tree; the sun was shining in, causing the tree's shadow to fall across William's leg. He looked down at the dark area of his pants leg for a while, then finally got up and walked slowly over the thick carpet and to the door Nan had gone through. Beyond the kitchen was a pantry, a washing machine against one wall with a hose running out of it and into a sink. On the edge of the sink William could see Nan's hand. He looked at her fingers for a while, then turned around and walked back.

At the same dinner party that Nan Morris told William what house he should live in, Chester Morris told him what job he should take.

It was toward the end of the evening. The four of them were having a small glass of cognac together when Chester asked William what his job prospects were. He replied that he had none but was soon going to apply for work in personnel departments for a beginning. Chester suggested he consider taking up the sale of stocks and bonds. William said it hadn't occurred to him before, but he was open to suggestions. Chester then wrote down the name of a broker whom he'd recently been in touch with, who'd mentioned his firm was looking for intelligent young men. William took the piece of paper and thanked him.

The next day he drove into a brokerage house in Los Angeles and had coffee with the man whose name was on the slip of paper. The man told him he had real potential as a stockbroker, just from their brief talk, and William said the job wasn't out of the question. The man said it would be best if he could go east for a training program, but if that was impossible there was a training program right in Los Angeles which was just as good.

That night William discussed the idea with Lisa. She didn't want to go back east but otherwise had no objections to his being a stockbroker. He told his mother; she said she didn't know what it had to do with psychology or his other interests. Nothing, he said. Then he explained to her that he was entering a new phase of his life, a more serious phase, and couldn't be thinking of psychology any more.

William didn't do as well as some of the others in the training class, although he got all the way through. (Three dropped out for reasons that were never announced to the others, although one of the drop-outs stood up in the second class session and told the teacher the entire business system in the nation was based on fraud, hypocrisy and anti-humanitarianism. As the other classmate was making his remarks William listened and thought to himself that it seemed to be true what the person was saying, but the other person probably had something else to do, which William didn't, so William stayed.)

After the course ended William was assigned to a desk. It was near the center of a row of desks. There were two rows in back of his, and two in front, with the large electrical quotation board overhead at the front of the room.

On William's desk was a telephone, with buttons on it under the dial, and a large brown blotter in a holder with a strip of light brown leather at each side. The desk was well-polished and had always been dusted before he came to work every morning.

For his first few weeks one of the senior brokers helped William out. Then, after he had a few clients, he was put on his own. As he had learned in the training course (and written down at more than one place in his notebook) the broker who is not aggressive is not a broker for long. So his first days were spent calling people he'd never heard of before and asking if they would like the names of a few stocks to follow, which his firm was recommending. In addition to not getting any new clients, he lost four of those the senior broker had helped him get, but he didn't tell any of the others. Instead he lied to them, saying all was going well.

During his third or fourth week at the brokerage William had a very bad time. He found that he felt a heavy and unrelieved feeling of depression, worse than any he could ever remember feeling. He knew it was because he hadn't sold anyone any stocks yet, and he thought a lot about the person who stood up to say the business system was hypocritical, wishing he'd had that person's courage. He also thought about taking a personality-improvement course on the side, because he knew one reason he wasn't succeeding was that he wasn't being forceful enough or in any way positive with the prospective customers (in fact on one of his worst days a lawyer he had called had to ask him several times over the phone to speak up because he couldn't hear him, then at the end of the conversation told him he didn't know much about William's company but hoped the other salesmen had more on the ball than he did).

It was during the lunch hour after the lawyer's conversation that William went down a few blocks to a bar and got drunk. He was late getting back, but by that time he didn't care. He walked in to his desk, banging against the backs of several of the other brokers' swivel chairs, and sat down. He didn't care what happened, because he had realized in the bar that it didn't matter if he succeeded as a stockbroker or not—this wasn't the most important thing and to worry so much about it as he had that week was bad for his health and could ultimately lead to nervous or digestive disorders.

So he sat at his desk, the other brokers phoning or milling about around him, the old men, mostly unkempt, wandering in off the street to sit in the chairs in the front and look up at the large quotation board overhead, even though it had been turned off since noon.

After a while, when he thought some of the others might be noticing that he was just sitting, he picked up the receiver of his phone, pretended to dial, then pretended he was speaking to someone, mentioning loudly the stocks his company recommended, sometimes gesturing with his pen as he spoke or opening a booklet in front of him to consult a figure, and sometimes leaning back in his swivel chair and laughing as though to a joke being told by the party on the other end. When he was finished he made some notations on a scratch pad, then sat back again in his chair, as though contemplating. He sat nearly an hour, then decided to call back the lawyer.

During the second phone call with the lawyer he wasn't drunk any more, but he wasn't quite sober either, and when he let himself think about it he became aware that the heartburn was starting which was always an inevitable and highly unpleasant side-effect he suffered when he drank anything alcoholic.

What he said to the lawyer was that his name was William Alren and he was employed by E. F. Hutton, a brokerage in downtown Los Angeles. He said it quite loudly, so the man would be sure and hear. When he was finished saying it there was a long silence, then the lawyer replied that he had already called him before that day. Pulling a sheet of figures toward him, William mentioned three stocks that the research department felt would perform quite well in the course of the next several months. He suggested the lawyer make a note of them and see how they did. Instead of answering, though, the lawyer hung up the phone, but by that time William knew he was going to make it in the American business community after all.

Through the living room window William watched as Nan and Chester met in the center of the lawn and kissed; then he got up and started for the front hallway.

"Well, here he is now," Chester said stepping through the door. He held out his hand and William shook it. When they were finished Chester put a manila folder down on the hall table. "It looks like you picked up a little color down there."

"Some." William looked down at his arm.

"Nan and I have to get down and visit you for a day. Excuse me a minute, will you?"

"Of course."

"Would you like a drink?"

"No thank you."

Chester turned in a circle. "Nan?"

"I'm phoning," she said from the other room, "can you wait?"

"How's Mark."

"Better, but he still has to stay in bed."

Chester turned back toward William. "Mark has the flu."

"Now that you're home," William said, "I wonder if I could go in and see Lisa."

"Lisa?"

"I understand my wife Lisa's been your guest here two nights," he said. "Now that you're home, what if I went back and said hello to her."

"Of course. Why not."

"No reason why not," William said. "It's just that your wife didn't want me to see her till you got home."

"Why didn't she."

"She didn't say why," William said. "Being your house, though, I thought I'd wait till you gave the okay."

"Oh."

"Do you give it?"

"Of course."

"I'll go find her."

Nan stepped out from around a wall with a telephone receiver up to her ear. "Just a minute, Bill, could you?" She waved her hand at her husband. "Chester? Could I see you?"

"What's up here."

"It's just that Lisa and I had an extremely good talk this afternoon. We figured a lot out together. Before Bill sees her I thought you and he should have a talk."

"About what," Chester said.

Nan disappeared back around the wall and began talking into the telephone.

"About what," Chester said to William.

"I don't know."

Chester looked down at the carpet, then back at William. "Have you been here long?"
"Half an hour."
It was quiet a few moments, then Chester walked into the dining room so he could see his wife. "Dear, what are Bill and I supposed to talk about."
She waved him back into the living room.
"I'll go get Lisa now," William said.
"Don't let him, dear."
"Bill," Chester said, gesturing at a chair against the wall, "let's sit down here. Maybe when Nan gets off the phone we can figure out what she has in mind for us."
William looked down at the chair.
"Sit down, sit down."
"How about this: why don't you come back with me while I see her."
Chester stepped into the dining room. "What if I went back with Bill to see Lisa."
"Fine," Nan said, "fine; you do that."
"I think that would satisfy all parties concerned," Chester said as he stepped back into the living room.
"Good. Who wants to go first."
"Shall I?"
"Go ahead."
Chester led the way out of the living room and down a hallway toward the rear of the house. "She's been staying in the guest room."
"I thought she probably had."
Half way down Mark opened his door and stuck out his hand. "Hi, Bill," he said.
"How are you doing."
Chester tousled his head as he went past him. "Glad to hear you're better."
"I'm not." He closed the door.
When he got to the end of the hall Chester stopped, tilted his head slightly, then knocked.
"Yes?"
"It's Chester and Bill," he said.
"Come in."

Chester turned back toward William. "Maybe you could . . ." He nodded at the door. "Go on—I'll wait out here."

"You're sure."

"Go on, Bill."

He turned the doorknob and pushed the door part way open.

"You're sure Nan wouldn't . . ."

"You go right in, Bill."

Suddenly the door opened the rest of the way and Lisa stood in front of them.

"Ah," Chester said. "How are you holding up, sister-in-law."

"Fine," she said. "How was work."

"Busy."

It was quiet for several moments till finally William cleared his throat and turned toward Chester. "Maybe if we could be alone just a minute."

"Sure, Bill."

William stepped in through the door. "Thank you. I'll leave the door ajar."

"Come on down for a drink when you get ready."

"Thank you, Chester." William closed the door most of the way, then turned toward Lisa again.

She walked across the room to a small dressing table against the wall, then seated herself on an upholstered bench in front of it.

"Is this your room?"

"It's the guest room."

William glanced at a flower in the pattern of the wallpaper, then at Lisa again. "You might have heard Nan and me talking in the living room."

"I heard your voices."

"She wanted me to wait till Chester came home before coming back here."

Lisa looked down at the glass top of the dressing table. There were several bobby pins lying on the center of it. She picked one up and turned it in her fingers.

"So." William stood a few moments longer beside

the door, then walked to an armchair in the corner and seated himself. "So," he said. "I'm here."

She continued looking down at the bobby pin in her hand.

"I say 'I'm here,' Lisa."

"I know you're here, William."

He ran his hand back and forth on the arm of the chair.

"Are you here for dinner?"

"I think there's a standing invitation."

Lisa turned around on the seat so she was facing a mirror up over the dressing table. "Were you invited to spend the night?"

"No."

"Would you like me to have Nan ask you for the night?"

"That would be kind of you," he said. "I hadn't thought of it."

She leaned closer to the mirror and inspected her lips.

"Had *you* planned to spend the night here?" he said.

"Yes."

He nodded.

"I'm having my vacation," she said.

"I know," he said. "How is your vacation."

"Fine." She turned around on the seat.

"Would you like me to talk to the psychiatrist?"

"That's up to you."

"I'll talk to him," William said. "Shall I?"

She looked down at one of her knees, then crossed it over the other one.

"Would that help?"

She shook her head.

He walked toward her, then got down on one of his knees in front of the seat. "I hadn't planned for it to be like this when I got up here," he said. "I'd planned to be a little more forceful." He looked up as the door opened.

"I don't mean to be a bother," Nan said, smiling in at him, "would you like to stay over tonight, Bill?"

"I haven't thought that far ahead."

"You can have the extra bed in Mark's room if you'd like," she said. "He's just getting over a little flu, but I'm sure you won't bother each other." She stepped out and closed the door.

"Lisa," he said, resting his hand on her knee.

Nan opened the door again. "Did Lisa tell you about the concert?"

"What concert is that."

"The three of us were going to a concert at eight thirty. I've just called the auditorium and they have no more seats. If you'd really like to see it I'll give you my ticket."

"Oh, no."

"Whatever you want," she said, stepping back and closing the door again.

"Lisa."

Again the door opened. William got to his feet as Nan looked in. "By the way," she said, "I just talked to Dr. Sadler too. He wants to stop by and meet Bill. I'll call you when he comes." She stepped out and closed the door.

"I guess you have no choice about seeing the doctor," Lisa said.

"Have you told him things about us?"

"Yes."

"What things."

"Just the things that occurred to me."

"Could I ask what they were?" he said. "I'd like to know before I meet him."

"Just my feelings."

"About what."

She turned to face the mirror again and pinned her hair back over her ear. "I told him I feel dissatisfied with myself, my life, my marriage—I told him the kind of things you tell psychiatrists."

William sat down beside her on the seat. "Do you want me to tell you I love you. If it's important I'll tell you as often as you want."

"If it makes you feel better."

"It doesn't make *me* feel better," he said, "but does it make *you* feel better."

"To hear it?"

"Yes."

She shook her head.

"So I won't say I love you all the time. You'll just know it."

"How will I." She picked up a bobby pin.

"You'll know it," he said, "because I'll tell you now and you'll remember it."

She pinned some hair up over her forehead.

"Lisa," he said, staring at her face in the mirror, then turning to look at her real face, "I'm trying very hard to break through."

"Through what."

"This." He waved his hand between their faces. "This mist. This vapor."

She lowered her hands to her lap and looked at him. "This what?"

"This gulf."

"What gulf."

"This one," he said, getting up, hitting his hip against the dressing table. "Here." He gestured at the space between them. "Do you see, Lisa."

"You're trying to break through a gulf."

"Our gulf."

"I hope you succeed."

"I intend to."

She looked at him a moment longer, then stood. "Excuse me." She walked toward the door.

"Lisa?"

"It's Nan's and Chester's custom to have a drink about now," she said. "I usually join them."

"Could you turn around?"

"What for."

"Just for a minute," he said. "I'd like you to just turn around for a minute."

She waited a moment, then turned around and looked at him. "What is it."

"Tell me what you think about," he said. He took a step toward her. "Can you?"

Lisa frowned.

"Think about," he said. "Think." He pointed at his head.

"When."

"Just here," he said, pointing down at the seat, "what you were thinking about just as we were sitting here beside each other."

She shrugged.

"What was it."

She glanced at the seat, then at William. "I don't understand; are you trying to be the psychiatrist?"

"No," he said, "but if you answer I think we'll be able to start." He took another step toward her. "I just have a feeling—that's what it will take to start."

"What I was thinking about on the seat?"

"Yes."

"I don't remember."

"You do, Lisa."

She reached for the doorknob but William walked toward her and removed her hand.

"Is this what you came up here to do? To try and provoke a scene?"

"You do remember what you were thinking about on the seat, don't you."

"Yes."

"But you don't want to tell me, do you."

"No."

"But I'm asking you to," he said, leading her back toward the seat, "that's all I'm asking you to do."

She removed her hand from his.

"Lisa?"

"My thoughts aren't your business."

"I'm making them my business, Lisa. From now on."

"How can my thoughts be your business."

He moved around between her and the door. "Just tell me what you were thinking."

"I won't."

He locked the door. "You will," he said, "before you leave this room."

"I'd say this psychiatrist is coming none too soon," she said. "Now open the door."

He shook his head.

"Yes, William."

"What are you thinking right now."

She started toward the door but he pressed his back against it.

"Just tell me, Lisa; then you can go out."

"I'm thinking that I hate you."

He nodded.

"Now let me out."

"You hate me," he said. "Why."

"I don't know," she said. "I don't care, but I'm sick of you, I'm through with you, and I hate you."

"And what are you going to do about it."

"I'm going to get out."

"Of the room?"

"Of the room," she said, "of your life, of the marriage."

"And do what."

She shook her head.

"I want you to tell me what your plan is," he said, "the specific plan. You have one, don't you."

"Yes."

"You've never told me about it, have you."

"No."

"Have you ever told anyone?"

"No."

"But you have a fantasy in your mind of a better life, don't you."

"It's not a fantasy."

"It's a fantasy," he said, "and you go through the days thinking about this other life. Shall I tell you how I know that?"

"I don't care how you know."

"I know you have it because I do the same thing. I'm going to tell you what my fantasy is."

"I don't care what yours is."

"My fantasy is that I'm going to go up to Alaska someday and homestead and live with native women up there. Since we've been married that's something I've thought about every day. I've seriously thought it was something I would do, break away and do, when I got the courage up. Today I realized it was a fantasy and has nothing to do with reality. Now I want to know yours."

She shook her head.

"You know mine," he said. "I want to know yours."

"I don't have one."

"You do," he said. "You were thinking of it on the seat; I could tell. It's something you've always had. Just tell me this: why won't you tell me."

"Because it's not a fantasy," she said, "it's a plan."

"Tell me your plan."

"You can't stop me, William."

"I don't want to."

"You think you can," she said. "You think I'll tell you and you'll stop me."

"I won't stop you."

"No one can stop me."

"No one will stop you if it's what you really want."

"It is."

"Then no one can stop you."

"And I've started," she said. "I have letters."

"What letters."

She walked to a small table between the twin beds and pulled out its drawer. "Four letters," she said, removing four long air-mail envelopes. "So you see it's not a fantasy."

"May I see the letters?"

"Not if you're going to tear them up."

He held out his hand. "Here."

She waited a moment, then handed them to him. "You see, it's not a fantasy."

William began opening the first one but she reached out and removed them again from his hand. "You don't have to read them; just so you see they exist."

"They're from modeling schools."

"That's right, Bill."

"I just saw the first two. Are they all from New York?"

She returned them to the drawer. "They're all from New York, Bill, and I've been accepted at all four."

"You're going."

"Of course I'm going. As soon as I have the money I'm going to New York and enroll in one."

"Which one."

"I haven't decided."

"Would you like me to loan you the money?"

"No."

"How else will you get it."

"Somehow."

"Have you told Nan the idea?"

"No."

"Anyone?"

"No."

"Can I ask how long you've had the idea?"

"A long time," she said. "I used to think about it in high school; then I stopped thinking about it for a while, then recently I realized it's something I can do, something I have the talent and ability to do on my own, and nobody's going to stop me."

"You're going to be a model."

She nodded.

"Do you know exactly what it is you'll be modeling?"

"No."

"High fashion?"

"I don't know."

"Ladies' undergarments?"

"You're ridiculing me," she said, "but that won't stop me."

"It's silly, Lisa."

"It's not silly," she said, "it's something I can do. I have the figure and the talent."

"You have a good figure," he said, "and you're talented and intelligent and attractive. But it's silly."

"No."

He opened the drawer. "I'm going to tear up your letters."

"You're not."

She reached for them but William pulled them out of the drawer, quickly tore them in half, then tore them again and let the pieces fall on the floor.

Lisa turned suddenly and stared at him. "God, I hate you," she said, speaking through her teeth. "I'd give anything I have just to let you know how much I hate you."

"I love you, Lisa," he said, "and that's why I'm never going to let you go away from me. I don't know what it will take. If I have to leave my job I'll leave it. If I have to move I'll move. No matter what it is I'll do it. Nothing else matters to me, you're the only thing I love, and if it takes my whole life to somehow show that to you then that's how I'll spend it."

Lisa looked down at the pieces of paper on the floor.

William got down on his knees and began gathering them up. "If you want to be a model in New York I'll get you more applications. If you still want to in a week or ten days then we'll move back there so you can do it. I'm promising you that."

Lisa seated herself on the edge of the bed.

When the last piece of paper had been gathered William sat down beside her, holding the torn letters in his lap. "Lisa?"

"I don't know what I want, Bill."

"That doesn't matter."

"I go crazy," she said. "One minute I'm thinking I want to be a model, then I realize how stupid it is. The next minute I begin thinking I want to have a baby. Then it's the modeling again. Back and forth." She turned to look at him. "It's been that way every day for a year, Bill. Every day going crazy like that."

"I know."

"And I still don't know which."

"I know the feeling."

"What if I have a baby and then decide I should have gone into modeling instead."

"If you do," he said, "then we'll get a baby sitter. But I'm telling you that it can start to work out now between us."

"And how do you know."

"I just do."

"And you think of Alaska?"

"I think of making a cabin, a log cabin, clearing some woods and making one. Then of having native women come needing a place to stay when it gets cold."

"Lots of them?"

"Quite a few."

"Orgies?"

He nodded. "Not really Eskimo women," he said. "Not with parkas. Not dirty. Just sort of dark complected, coming out of the woods to me."

"Wearing clothes?"

"No," he said. "Maybe a couple of them wearing garments made out of reindeer hides."

Lisa looked down at the rug. "We're screwed up."

"I don't think we are though."

"I think of being on the cover of *Vogue* and you think of having sex orgies with Eskimos. What kind of a marriage is that."

"It's probably a normal one," William said, "but I think we can do better."

There was a knock, then the door opened and Nan's face appeared. "Dr. Sadler's coming up the walk." Just as she finished speaking three chimes rang in the front hall.

William gestured for Lisa to go out first, then followed the two girls down the hall. Nan reached the front door just before her husband did and opened it. A man in a suit was standing on the doormat. "Come in, Doctor."

He did.

"Bill?"

William stepped forward.

"I want you to know Dr. Sadler."

The doctor held out his hand. "This is a great pleasure." They shook hands.

"Of course you know Lisa," Nan said, "and this is my husband, Chester Morris." Chester shook the doctor's hand. "Shall we all sit down?" Nan said, leading the way to the living room. She gestured at the couch. "Doctor?"

"Thank you." He seated himself and William sat down beside him. It was quite a moment, then the doctor cleared his throat and turned to William. "I understand you've been down at the beach."

William was looking down at the ashtray on the table. "Yes," he said.

"How was it."

He nodded. "Very nice."

"I'd sure like to be down there right now."

"What was your name again?" William said, turning to look at him.

"Craig Sadler."

"And you're a psychiatrist."

"Yes."

"And this is a house call you're making."

"You mean . . ."

"A house call," William said. "Nan called you to come out here on a house call."

"Yes."

"Fine," William said. "Maybe I'm not supposed to ask this, but who's going to get the bill for it."

The doctor looked down at the ashtray. "Well . . ."

"Bill," Nan said, leaning forward on her chair.

"That can be taken care of," the doctor said. "Right

now why don't we try and get acquainted a little."

"But who's going to pay for our getting acquainted."

Suddenly Nan got up from her chair and walked to the entrance way of the dining room. "Bill? Will you come here please? Something I wanted to ask you about dinner."

William looked at the doctor a moment longer, then got up from his chair and walked toward the dining room. "What," he said.

"Could you come in the dining room please."

They stepped out of sight behind the wall.

"Bill," she said, "after all the good feeling we've built up between the doctor and Lisa, I won't have you talk to him this way in our house."

William looked at her a few moments, then turned around again.

"Bill?"

He stopped.

"Please come back here."

Again he turned around and stepped back in front of her.

"Did you hear what I said."

"I did," he said, "but there are some fundamental questions that no one else is raising."

She stared at him a moment, then stepped back to the entrance way of the living room. "Chester?"

Chester got up and joined them. "Will you please talk some sense to this person," she whispered. "I can't reason with him."

"Dear," Chester said, "you should have told us before you called the doctor over here."

"He said to call the minute Bill got here."

"Excuse me please." William stepped between them and back down into the living room. "What are your rates," he said, seating himself again beside the doctor.

"There's a standard fee of course."

"What is it."

The doctor cleared his throat. "It would be fifty-five dollars for each half hour, on a house call."

"Come on."

"Bill," the doctor said, turning toward him, "I must ask you to put these considerations aside for the moment. Will you?"

"I will," he said, "as soon as I find out who's going to pay."

"If you're able to pay," the doctor said, patting his knee, "I'll have my secretary send you the bill."

"It's me then."

"If you're able."

William nodded. "I am."

"Good. Now."

"Again," William said, leaning back into the cushion, "it might not be the right thing to ask, but I wonder if you could tell me what I'm going to get for my money."

"Get?"

"My fifty-five dollars for the half hour," he said. "What should I be expecting in return, if it's all right to ask."

"Of course it is." The doctor placed his hands together in his lap.

"Do I need to be sitting here for all this?" Lisa said. "I said I'd help get dinner."

"Maybe we could call her back when we straighten out some of these initial problems," William said.

Lisa got up and walked out of the room.

"Now," the doctor said, rearranging himself slightly, "let me say just one thing: you seem serious to know in advance what you'll get for your money."

"I am."

He nodded. "Yes," he said. "Fine. Then let me say this. For me to try and give you a point-by-point description of what you'll be getting would be out of the question. And I'll tell you why."

William reached for one of the cigarettes on the table.

"If successful," the doctor said, "you'll experience some peace of mind. Troublesome elements in your relationship with your wife will come clear to you."

William lit the cigarette.

"But as far as itemizing . . ."

William took a puff from the cigarette. "I'm sorry. I'd like to go on with the group discussion or whatever you had in mind."

The doctor looked down into his lap. "As you wish."

"Let me get the others." William got up, walked into the dining room and to the door of the kitchen. "The doctor and I have had an understanding," he said. "Could everyone come back please?"

Nan put down a potholder. Lisa put down a glass of water and they walked back across the room. Chester followed and William led the way back into the living room. "Where should we sit," William said.

The doctor made a large gesture with both his arms. "Where you please."

William gestured at the couch. "Nan?"

She walked past him and sat down.

"Chester?"

He walked to a chair by the wall and seated himself.

Lisa sat down on the couch on the other side of the psychiatrist, then William sat down in a chair. "Sorry," he said. "Nan, sorry."

She smiled.

"Now," the doctor said, "suppose we start by asking if there's anything anyone would like to say. Just anything. Anything at all." He looked over at William, who shook his head.

"Anyone?"

"No," Lisa said.

"Fine." The doctor pulled his pants legs up slightly and moved forward on the sofa. "Chester?" he said. "Suppose you tell us what you did today."

"When," Chester said.

"Did you go to the bank today?"

"Oh," he said, "yes."

"Can you tell us a little of what you did today at the bank?"

Chester looked down at the coffee table. "I worked," he said. "Let's see. Yes, well it was mostly processing a loan today." He looked back up at the doctor.

"Processing a loan," he said. "And can you tell us anything about this loan."

"Hmmm," he said. "Let's see." He reached for a cigarette. "It was to a construction company, a contractor. They want to put up an apartment building."

"Very good," the doctor said, "very good." He turned to face William.

"Yes?"

"What do you think of that."

Chester was leaning forward over the table, trying to reach the lighter. William handed it to him. "What do I think of what."

"What Chester just told us."

"The loan?"

"Yes."

"It sounded good," William said. "Fine."

"It didn't cause you any anxiety to hear what he said then."

William shook his head. "No."

"Good," the doctor said. "Would you like to tell us what you did today?"

William looked down as Chester returned the lighter to the table.

"When."

"I don't know. I take it you woke up this morning."

"Yes."

"Was it early?" the doctor said. "Late?"

William studied the table. "Late," he said. "Nine."

"That's late for you," the doctor said, "isn't it. Being a stockbroker, when do you usually have to get up."

"Six."

"And drive over to Los Angeles?"

"Yes."

"That's awfully early," the doctor said. "Does it bother you?"

William glanced across the table at Nan.

"Does it . . ."

"No," he said, "it doesn't. At first it did, but now I'm used to it."

"I guess you have to get there early because the stock market back in New York opens three hours earlier than the one here."

"That's the reason."

Nan was leaning slightly forward, looking from one person to the other as they spoke.

"So. Getting back to this morning. After rising around nine, did you then dress?"

Nan turned her head, awaiting William's response.

"Did you dress immediately upon rising, Bill?"

It was quiet.

"Well. Maybe you'd rather not answer that."

"It's not that," he said, "but I'd like to know why, if I may."

"Why what."

"Why you'd want to know if I dressed immediately after I got up this morning."

The doctor held up his hand. "Let's go on. Lisa?" He turned in his seat to look at her.

"Wait," William said. "I'm not trying to be uncooperative."

"I realize that."

"But I'm very sincerely trying to figure out what's the point of all this. Now is there a reason you want to know if I got dressed when I got up?"

"We're just talking," the doctor said. "We're just sitting here talking to each other."

"We're not just talking."

"Let's pass on," the doctor said. "Lisa?"

"Yes?"

"May I ask you a question."

She nodded.

William glanced again at Nan. She was sitting with her legs crossed and her hands in her lap, smiling.

"Lisa," the doctor said, "did anything happen to you today you'd like to tell us about?"

She looked down at the rug.

"Did you go out of the house?"

"Yes."

"And where did you go when you went out of the house."

"To your office."

"Oh yes."

Lisa nodded.

"And did your husband come up from the beach today?"

"Yes."

Suddenly William reached forward to grind out his cigarette. "We're going to have to go."

"Who is," Nan said.

"I am," he said, "and Lisa."

The doctor held out his hands. "Let's all see how calm we can . . ."

William looked over at his wife. "Did you unpack your suitcase from this morning?"

"You see, doctor," Nan said, getting up, "this is what she's up against, all the time."

William stood. "Is your suitcase still packed, Lisa."

"No."

The Doctor got to his feet. "Let's all sit down and explore what's happening here."

"Get up, Lisa," William said.

The doctor began motioning for everyone to go back down into their seats. "Now we're getting somewhere."

"Lisa." He motioned for her to stand.

"Do you see, Doctor?" Nan said, pointing at William "Can you imagine living day in and day out with an unstable personality like this?"

"Get up, Lisa."

"See how he threatens her," Nan said. "I'd like to tell you some of the things he was saying to me before my husband came home."

William stepped in front of the doctor and took Lisa's wrist. He pulled her up from the couch. "Get your suitcase packed—be out here in five minutes."

The doctor rested his hand on William's arm. "This

is healthy," he said. He motioned for Nan to sit. "This is the healthiest thing that could have happened."

"Lisa. Pack."

"Chester," Nan said, "I think you'd better intervene here if you plan to."

Chester got to his feet. "Actually, I hadn't planned to."

"There's nothing wrong with asserting yourself when the situation calls for it," the doctor said, looking up at William, "but I'd like right now to ask you one question."

"Lisa," Nan said, reaching over to try and pull her wrist free, "just sit down again."

"Here's the question," the doctor said, "why do you act as though you're being threatened."

"Because I am." He yanked Lisa past the doctor and past Nan, then pulled her toward the doorway into the hall. "Five minutes," he said. He propelled her down the hallway toward the back.

"William?" Nan said. "If you have any idea of taking her with you . . ."

William pointed out toward the kitchen. "Go get your dinner."

"William, dear."

"Really," he said, "go get your dinner ready. We won't be staying. Go get your and Chester's dinner."

Nan looked over at the Doctor. "Do you see this kind of thing often, doctor: this kind of hysteria in a man?"

William grabbed Nan's shoulder, spun her around and pushed her up over the single step leading into the dining room. Then he pushed her through the swinging door into the kitchen.

"Chester!" she called.

"Get your dinner ready."

She wrenched free of him. "Get out."

"Get your and Chester's food."

"Get out of my kitchen."

Stuck to one of the doors of the stove was a large glove made out of a thick fireproof material, to be used as a potholder. William grabbed it. "Put this on." He took her hand and pushed the glove onto it.

"Chester?"

"Now!" He raised his arm. Then he turned as the swinging door opened and looked at Chester.

The three of them stood still for several moments, then very slowly William lowered his arm.

Nan straightened up and pulled off the glove. "There's nothing to say, Bill," she said. "I don't think I could ever hope to express to you the extreme disappointment your actions in the last few minutes are to me, disappointment in you as a human being, so I won't even try."

"I'd like to fix everyone a drink," Chester said. "It'll help us calm down. Bill?"

William nodded.

"What'll you have."

"Gin and tonic. . . . Thank you." He looked over at Nan.

"Let's not talk to each other any more today, Bill."

"I wasn't planning to."

She looked down at the bright flowered material of the glove in her hand. "You go wait for us—we'll bring the drinks in."

William turned around and walked past Chester and out the door, letting it swing closed as Chester dropped ice into a glass.

The doctor was still on the couch, sitting with his hands on the cushions beside him. He indicated one of the chairs and smiled. "I wasn't worried, Bill," he said.

"I'm sorry."

"Don't be," he said. "Now we know you're human like the rest of us."

It was quiet a moment, then William rested his hand on the back of the chair.

"The air's cleared now," Dr. Sadler said. "We've made a beginning."

William looked down at his wristwatch. "I was just

trying to remember," he said, "what time you got here."

"I?"

"You keep track, don't you, if you have to charge for your time."

"It was just twelve before six when I came."

"It's six fifteen now."

"Yes."

William removed his wallet from his back pocket. "I'd like to pay you," he said, "if it wouldn't mess up your bookkeeping." He removed several bills, then put his wallet back in his pocket. "Can you take it now?"

"If you'd like." He held out his hand.

"You can."

"Either way," the doctor said, "whatever's most convenient for you."

William seated himself slowly on the chair. He rested the bills over one of his knees.

"You know, Bill," the doctor said, leaning back on the sofa, "the first thing any good psychiatrist or counselor learns is that an individual has to want help before he can be helped."

"Is that right."

"He has to have the desire to be helped, you see."

"Then what," William said.

"Well. Once he sees that he *needs* help, then he can *be* helped."

"By you."

The doctor laughed.

"Helped by you."

"Yes."

"And you believe that."

The doctor stopped laughing and looked up at him.

"You really believe that you help other people," William said quietly. He glanced at the door of the kitchen.

Dr. Sadler cleared his throat. "Well I hope I do."

"You hope you do," William said, "but do you really . . . when it comes right down to it do you really believe you do."

The doctor reached for one of the cigarettes on the table. "Insofar as one individual is able to help another, yes."

"And how far is that." William handed him the lighter; the doctor lit the cigarette and set the lighter back on the table. "How far."

"What do you mean 'How far.' "

"Just that," William said.

"I help them explore some of their problems, perhaps in ways that hadn't occurred to them before." He crossed his legs and took a drag from the cigarette.

"What do you mean 'explore their problems.' "

"Look, we're playing word games."

"We're not."

"Well I hope we all know what problems are."

William shook his head.

"You don't?"

"What are they."

He reached forward to tap his cigarette in the ashtray. "Let's call them difficulties, resistances perhaps, that each of us encounters in our dealings with other individuals."

"And you remove them."

"No," he said, raising the cigarette to his mouth again, "I merely throw light on them."

"What kind of light."

He took a drag from the cigarette and blew smoke out over William's head. "If successful," he said. "I help to show the patient a new and more creative way of looking at them."

"But what way is it," William said. "It's your way. It's a way you've been taught. The method of psychiatry you've been taught in your school and your journals."

"Yes," he said, tapping his cigarette over the ashtray again, "but I would hope it has some correspondence to reality."

"Does it?"

"As I say, I would hope so."

"But does it?"

The doctor looked down at the cushion beside him. "Of course I couldn't say with utter certainty that it did."

"You couldn't."

"Of course not."

"So it might have little or nothing to do with the real facts of a person's life, this method."

"May I ask what branch of the science we're discussing?"

"I don't think that's important. But it might be an artificial system, not relevant to a person's life."

The doctor continued looking down at the cushion.

"Is that possible."

"I suppose it might."

William picked up the bills off his knee. "You have to make a living, don't you," he said.

"Of course."

"And you make it by doing this thing with people. Lying them on the couch, or sitting them in the chair, then doing this thing you've been trained to do."

The doctor leaned forward to grind out his cigarette. "I'm not sure I'd put it quite that way."

"But I think it would have been better if you had."

The doctor shook his head. "I don't see my profession that way. I think you're something of an anti-humanist in outlook. That may explain your . . ."

"Instead of coming in here and pretending you can help us . . . instead of getting my wife all excited about a newer, better life, getting my sister-in-law all worked up over problems that aren't any of her business, prying away at me over trivialities related to my daily routine, instead of all this why not just say you need to make a living, and you've learned this thing you can do with other people, and for fifty-five dollars a half hour you'll show us how you do it."

He looked up into William's face. "I'm not a trained seal, sir."

William held out the money. "I don't want to comment on that, but I'm asking you to leave now, before the others come back in."

Dr. Sadler looked over at the door of the kitchen.

"If I wasn't paying for your half hour I wouldn't have the right to ask you to leave, but I am paying, and I am asking you to go." He held the money closer to the doctor. "Here."

The doctor turned his head to look at the bills, then took them.

"Leave now, before we get into the next half hour." William stood. "Get up, Doctor."

He rose from the couch.

"I apologize for anything I've said that offended you. I came up from the beach because there's something I have to do here; I don't know what it is yet or how to do it. But it's the four of us—it's between me, Lisa, Nan and Chester." He motioned toward the door; the two of them started toward it.

"Just let me say one thing more," the doctor said.

"No, I'm not going to." William opened the door for him. "Thank you for coming. Goodbye."

The doctor looked up at him.

"Goodbye, Doctor."

Dr. Sadler stepped out onto the doormat on the porch. William closed the door. He stood a moment with his hand on the knob, then turned around.

Lisa was at the far end of the hall, next to the door of the guest room. "I'm not going with you," she said.

He nodded.

"I'm not, Bill."

"I heard you."

They stood looking at each other a few moments longer, then William turned as Chester stepped to the entrance way of the living room. He was holding a tray of drinks. "Where's the doctor," he said.

"He left."

Nan appeared behind him. "Where's Dr. Sadler." She took a step into the living room, looked at the place on the sofa where the doctor had been sitting, then at William.

"He's gone," William said.

"I see that. Where."

Chester looked down at one of the glasses on the tray. "What should I do with his martini."

Nan walked quickly past William and to the front door. She pulled it open and looked out to the street.

William walked into the living room and to Chester.

"Yours is closest to me," Chester said.

He reached between two other glasses for his drink and lifted it up from the tray.

Chester set the tray of remaining drinks on the table. "Nannie?"

She closed the door and returned to the entrance of the room. "What did you say to him, Bill."

"I paid him and he left."

"And what did you say to him." She stepped down into the room.

"As he left?"

"Yes."

"Good night."

"And before that."

"I thanked him for coming."

Chester picked up a drink from the tray and carried it to Lisa, as she stepped into the room. Then he walked back to the tray and picked up another drink to carry toward his wife, but she walked past him and up to William. "What did you say to Dr. Sadler that made him leave."

"I asked him to leave."

"You did."

"I asked him nicely. I told him I appreciated his coming and asked him very politely to go."

Nan stared at him for several moments, then turned. "My drink."

"Here," Chester said, picking it up again and handing it to her.

She walked around the table and seated herself.

"Shall I put on a record?" Chester said.

She shook her head.

"I didn't feel we were accomplishing things with him here," William said. "Did you? Did anyone?" He looked at Lisa.

"I thought we were," Lisa said. She seated herself on the sofa beside her brother-in-law. "We were trying to get out our emotions in a controlled way," she said. "I think that was the point of it."

"Let's forget it," Nan said. She smiled. "Bill, sit down."

He seated himself.

"Chester?" Nan said to her husband, who was standing at the side of the table, holding two drinks. "Go throw Dr. Sadler's drink out."

"I'll put it in the icebox." He turned and left the room.

"He was trying to help us by getting us to talk to each other about everyday matters," Lisa said. "As a beginning. But I don't think he had a chance from the moment he stepped in the door."

"Let's forget it now," Nan said. "Chester, put on your record."

"May I say something?" Lisa said.

Chester walked up to a record player and lifted up a record jacket.

"What are you playing," Nan said.

"This." He turned the jacket to face her.

"Why that."

"It's quiet," he said, "soothing."

Nan got up and walked across the room. Holding the drink she looked down at the record cover. Then, finally, she turned around. "Bill," she said, "I'm going to ask you to leave now."

William looked back at her.

"I am," she said, "because your presence is too much of a strain. On me, on Lisa, and on Chester. It's as simple as that, and I'm terribly sorry, but you'll have to go now."

Chester looked down into his record player.

William continued looking across the room at Nan.

"I'm sorry," she said.

"All right."

"Will you go please?"

"Yes," he said. He took a sip of his drink. "Just one thing first."

"What is it."

He looked at Lisa, then back to Nan. "Lisa mentioned that she had something to say . . ."

"No," Nan said, walking back toward them, "you see, this is what your presence does—it makes us all very upset and we lose perspective and say things we don't mean."

"As soon as Lisa says what she wanted to say, I'll go."

Nan shook her head. "She doesn't have anything to say," she said. "We have dinner to eat." She glanced at her watch. "A concert at eight thirty. We'll have to get together another time for an intense emotional discussion, I'm not up to it now."

William turned toward his wife. "What did you have to say."

Suddenly loud violin music vibrated through the room from the record player in the corner. Chester quickly turned the volume down, then picked up his drink. "Let's have our drink," he said, walking back to his seat. "Let's just have our drink and not think of anything else for the moment." He raised his glass. "Here," he said. "A toast."

"To what," Nan said.

He looked at William, then at Lisa. "Let's just have our drink." He took a sip from it, then gestured at Nan's chair. "Sit down, honey. Bill," he said, "have I played this record for you before?"

"No."

"It's an all-girl French choir. We love it. Listen to the harmony."

William nodded.

Lisa said, "I would like Bill to have some dinner before he goes."

Nan turned to look at William. "You do what you want, Bill," she said. "I guess it's asking too much for you to have any regard for our feelings, our endurance. You see, we don't live on the intense emotional peak that you're used to."

"I'm not used to an intense emotional peak."

"You don't realize it," she said, "but we're basically just sort of average, ordinary people. We go along from day to day the best we can. As far as having a crisis suddenly dumped in our lap, we'll do our best to cope with it, but you'll just have to be patient with us."

"I don't think I dumped it there."

"I know you don't," she said, "and I'm doing my best to understand your reasoning and motivations, but for now you'll just have to try and accept our rather humdrum ways."

"Let's change the subject," Chester said.

William leaned forward in his chair. "I don't recall anyone accusing you of anything," he said. He waited a few moments, then moved back on his chair again. Chester was tapping the toe of one of his shoes to the music. Every several seconds as there was a high trilling note by some of the voices he moved his head briefly from side to side in time with the music. Lisa sat holding her drink, looking down at the cushion beside her. "What's the name of the choir," he said.

Nan held up her hand. "Let's just sit and listen."

"I just asked the name of the choir, Nan."

"Let me go get you the record jacket," Chester said.

Nan set her drink down on the table. "You see, this is what we're not used to in this house, Bill: this kind of chaos you seem to bring with you wherever you go."

"Should I not have asked the name of the choir?"

"To you, chaos is normal."

"To me, chaos is not normal."

Lisa got up from the couch. "Excuse me," she said.

"Are you going somewhere?" Nan said.

"My room." She stopped at the entrance of the dining room but then turned around and walked back to her seat and sat down again.

Chester carried the record cover across the room and handed it to William. He read part of it, then set it down on the table.

"What I wanted to say before," Lisa said, "is that I've decided to go away. I'm not sure when, or where, but if it will lessen some of the tension, I have plans to leave in the next few days."

Nan looked at her husband. "Go turn off the music. We have to think about dinner."

Chester sat where he was, whistling softly with the tune from the phonograph.

Nan took a final sip from her glass and stood. "Bill, are you staying or not."

"He's staying," Lisa said.

"That's four of us then. Lisa, you set the table. Bill, what could you do."

"I can't think here any more than I could at the beach," Lisa said.

"Where are you going this time," William said.

"I don't know yet." She took a last large swallow from her drink.

"I know what you could do, Bill," Nan said. "You can go out in the back yard and pick some mint leaves."

William carried his drink around the table to his wife. "Will you go to your parents' house this time?"

"No."

"New York?"

"Not right away," she said. "Just somewhere I can think."

"Lisa," he said, taking her hand and leading her to the couch, "let's sit down." He sat beside her.

Chester got up and walked to the record player. "I'll keep this very soft, but I want to hear the next band." He turned down the volume, then sat down on the rug with his drink.

William took a large swallow from his.

"Are you going to set the table, Lisa," Nan said.

"When dinner's ready."

Nan walked out of the room, hitting her elbow against the doorway as she went through it.

"What was I going to say," William said, still holding Lisa's hand.

"We're all drunk," Lisa said, "but I'm going to tell you something that's true. I'm going to tell you why I can't be with you, the real reason, and it's because I have no power when I'm with you," she said. "It's that simple."

William looked down at his knee.

"And there's no way you can give me any without destroying your own personality. That's why we're incompatible."

"You want power."

"I want the feeling I can make things happen."

"You have power over all the people in this house," he said. "You're making them all go nuts."

She removed his drink from his hand and raised it to her lips. "I want power over myself. If I had that, I'd be happy."

Nan returned to the room carrying Dr. Sadler's martini, the glass frosted from being in the icebox. "I just have one more thing to say before I dish out dinner," she said. She walked over to sit on the other side of William from Lisa. "As far as the mint leaves go," she said, "don't worry about it. We have mint jelly instead. Mint sauce is better made with fresh leaves, but mint jelly's fine when you've all had a strong drink." She reached for a cigarette. William picked up the lighter and lit it. "Thank you."

"You're welcome."

"You know, you're very thoughtful. You're a thoughtful person, Bill."

He nodded.

"Just the other day I was saying to myself, 'Bill Alren is one of the politest people I know—it seems like we should get along, but we don't even though he's polite.'" She took a drag from the cigarette. "Lisa, as we grew up, what did you think of me."

Lisa looked down at the table.

"She used to worship the ground I walked on," Nan said to William. "Really. Literally. She used to buy the same dresses and use the same expressions I did. I noticed it, but of course I didn't say anything. But as I think back I don't think it's healthy to have that kind of a dependency on an older sister." She took a sip from the martini. "I have to dish out dinner," she said, "but first I had one thing to say." She glanced over at Chester, seated on the rug beside the phonograph, the drink on the rug beside his shoe as he tapped to the music. "Chester and I," she said. "We're simple people, Bill, that's what you don't realize about us. We're not sophisticates; that's where you have us pegged all wrong."

"I never thought you were."

"Excuse me," she said. She got up and walked slowly out of the room.

"I have to have the feeling that everything I do is something I choose to do myself," Lisa said. "That's what I've never felt. And whoever I married, I would have left him, because whoever I married would have stood for someone making decisions for me. And I've reached a point in my life where that's not possible any more."

"I'll say one thing."

"It doesn't matter who you are. Anybody who tries to tell me anything from now on, that means Nan, you, anybody, I'm not going to listen. Only to myself will I listen from now on."

"That's good, Lisa."

"You say it's good," Lisa said, "but now you're going to tell me I'm wrong."

"You are."

"But I'm not listening."

"I know that," he said, reaching for a cigarette, "and you don't have to, but I'm just going to say it's important that we have our bodies in the same general physical area."

She turned to look at him. "Why are you smoking."

"I don't know." He picked up the lighter and lit the cigarette, then returned it to the table. "Our senses are what's important about our marriage," he said. "I'm the one who has to make the decisions; that's just how it is."

"Bill?" Chester called from across the room. "See if you can hear this high note."

"But we like thinking about each other. We like looking at each other and we like touching each other. We like hearing each other's voice. Even arguing. It's irrelevant whether we're arguing or agreeing, but there's something about each of us that responds to the other person's voice, just the sound of it. And that's why we can never stay apart."

"Hear that?" Chester said. He got up from the rug. "Let me play that over."

It was Chester's suggestion that wine be served with dinner, and just before everyone sat down he went into the basement and brought up a bottle, dusted it with a dish towel in the kitchen, opened it and carried it around the table, pouring some in each person's glass.

"None of us really know what's happening at all, do we," Lisa said as her glass was being filled with the red liquid.

Chester tipped the bottle up, then walked to the end of the table to fill his wife's glass.

"Do we," Lisa said.

William looked across the table at her. "To whom are you addressing your question."

"I'm saying that we're all going along, doing what we think we should, pretending we know what the reasons are, but when it comes down to it none of us do."

Chester poured William's glass nearly full, then walked to his own place at the table to pour his. "Where shall I put this," he said when he was through.

Nan pointed at a piece of furniture against the wall. "On the buffet." Chester carried the bottle to it and set it down.

"I still don't know who you're addressing," William said.

Lisa picked up her napkin and opened it in her lap.

"I think Lisa had a very strong drink," Nan said. She picked up her fork and cut the end off a broccoli spear on her plate.

Lisa turned toward Chester. "We're all here in this situation," she said, "aren't we."

"Where are our seats for the concert," Nan said. "Did you notice?"

"I didn't notice," Chester said.

"I'm just saying that we're all in a situation but none of us feel any control over it."

Chester pulled his napkin off the table and into his lap. "I'm not much of a philosopher, Lisa," he said, raising a bite of broccoli to his mouth, "but we should think of moving right along. Last time we had to park four blocks away from the auditorium."

Lisa turned toward her sister.

"I think you're a little tippy," Nan said. "I'll put this over here for a while." She picked up Lisa's wine glass and set it next to William's.

"I'm talking about control," Lisa said across the table to William. "Do you think any of us have it."

He cut a bite from a lamb chop on his plate. "Yes."

"Who."

"I think I have control over my bodily movements." He raised the bite to his mouth.

"This is getting too intellectual," Chester said. "Let's change the subject."

"I'm not talking about bodily movements," Lisa said. "I'm talking about control over events."

Nan turned toward William and studied his plate for a few moments. "You didn't get much of a potato," she said, "let me trade with you."

"This one's fine."

She speared her own baked potato with her fork, lifted it over to William's plate, shook it off, then speared his and brought it back to her own plate.

"I'm talking," Lisa said, "about . . ."

Nan turned to her. "We know what you're talking about," she said. "Why don't you take it up with your pastor next Sunday morning." She picked up her knife and sliced open her baked potato. "It's not a topic for the dinner table."

"Why not."

"Because it's boring."

"But what degree of control do we have over our own lives, that's what I'm asking." She held her hand across the table. "May I have my wine back please."

William handed it to her.

"Why did I come up here from the beach," Lisa said. "Was it *my* decision? Or something that was inevitable, given the circumstances." She took a sip from the wine.

"It was your decision," William said.

"Was it though."

He nodded.

Nan stuffed a large slice of butter down into the crack of her baked potato. "Whose decision did you think it was."

"It doesn't seem like it was mine any more."

"Well it wasn't mine."

"It seems like I didn't have any choice."

William split open his potato with his fingers. "May I have the butter." Nan passed him the butter. "You always have a choice," he said, "everything you do you have a choice. You make it, then you go ahead."

"I don't believe that."

"You don't have to." He cut off some butter. "That doesn't alter the fact that it's true."

"How do you know."

"By observing."

Chester held out his hand. "Bill, I'll have that butter down here."

William handed it to him.

"Do you feel you have complete control over what you do," Lisa said to her sister.

"Yes, dear."

"You do?"

"I would have to agree with Bill that I make my choices and go ahead. If you don't, then that's your business, but you're too old to be bringing this up at a dinner table. It's an adolescent thing to discuss."

"It's unsophisticated."

Nan reached for her wine. She took a sip, then returned it to the tablecloth, just above her teaspoon. "That's right."

Chester was cutting some meat off the bone of his lamb chop. "Do you feel you have control over the things that happen to you?" Lisa asked.

He set down the bone and lifted the bite of meat to his mouth. "Certainly we don't control the weather conditions."

"Do you control your moods?"

Chester looked at his wine glass a few moments. "No," he said finally.

"Are you controlling the fact that Bill is here eating with you?"

Chester glanced at William. "I'm happy to have him here."

"But why is he here?"

"I guess he needs a meal," Chester said, reaching for his glass. "Right, Bill?"

"But we're all here in this room, aren't we."

Nan tapped her butter knife against her glass. "Lisa."

"Just tell me this," Lisa said. "What bothers you about my saying 'we're all here in this room.' "

Nan began cutting her lamb chop. "In case you hadn't gathered, Bill," she said, "Lisa was a philosophy major at Mills."

"I know."

"And she's getting some things off her chest. She's been thinking about things, that was her intention in coming here. It's good. Just let her go on."

Chester set his napkin on the table beside his plate and pushed back his chair. "More wine, Bill?"

William spent the evening quietly. When the others had gone he found a magazine on the living room table and leafed slowly through it. Then he walked into the den. He seated himself in an armchair and turned on the television with a remote control switch. He turned around to the different channels, watched a girl in a shoulderless gown sing a song, then picked up a newspaper from the table beside him. He looked at the front page, then turned to the financial page. He looked up several stocks, then folded the paper and set it on the table. He turned off the television, then got up and walked into the hall. He sat down on a chair beside a telephone, looked up a number in the phone book, then dialed the phone and waited till a lady answered.

"Mrs. Peterson," he said, "this is William Alren calling. I have the paper here on my lap and I see that Atlantic's gone down another six points since we last talked."

"Aren't you on vacation?" she said.

"I am," he said, "but I knew you'd have some questions about the situation."

"I do."

"I thought you might," he said. "Now I'm going to tell you to still hold on, Mrs. Peterson, even though we might see the stock go down another point or two this week."

"May I say something?" she said.

"Yes."

"May I say two things."

"Go on."

"That stock and the small amount I have in the savings account is the only money I have, you know that."

"I do," William said, "and that's why I'm calling, even though it's my vacation."

"And sixty-two dollars a month from the Social Security."

"Mrs. Peterson."

"Now may I say something else?"

William settled back a little farther in the chair.

"Before your vacation you said the stock would hold steady till you got back."

"I thought it would."

"Yes," she said, "but this isn't your money—it's mine."

"It's your money," he said, leaning forward again, "and I plan to help you make it grow."

"Well yes, that's what you keep saying."

"Mrs. Peterson," he said, "would you like me to explain again what's happening and why we can look for a solid recovery within the next six weeks."

"Why."

"Because the strike is having a longer term effect than our research department anticipated. Remember I told you there was a strike against the company last month?"

"And I said I wanted to get out."

"And I told you it was only the nervous investor who was going to get scared out now: and he'd be hurt the most by getting out. But the wise investor is going to stay put, Mrs. Peterson, because he knows when the strike's over he's going to see some growth."

There was a long silence. "Why is the strike still on."

"There's been a settlement," William said, "but four local unions are still holding out; it's called wildcatting when a few isolated branches hold out for a while against the policy of their union, but they always come back in line and then the strike's over."

"I don't understand this."

"You don't have to," William said. "Just take my word for it that all the big money's staying put."

"What about the little money."

"I know the situation. Our research department knows the situation. The minute there's any cause for concern you'll know. Okay?"

"Couldn't you sell me a stock that went up, instead of down?"

"As soon as I'm back in the office," William said,

"make an appointment and come in for an hour some afternoon. Have you heard from your son?"

"He's still in Spain."

"We'll make a date as soon as I'm back," William said. "If you have any more letters from him I hope you'll bring them by. It's been a pleasure talking to you."

"Thank you."

"Good night, Mrs. Peterson." William got up and walked down the hall to Mark's room. He opened the door quietly, noticed from the hall light where the door of the bathroom was, then closed the door and walked to the bathroom. He undressed and left his clothes on a clothes hamper, then walked slowly through the dark to the bed closest to the wall. He pulled down the covers and got in.

There was a squeaking of springs from the other bed. "Uh?" Mark said.

"It's me. Bill."

The light went on on the table between the two beds. William looked over to see Mark Morris squinting at him.

"I'm turning in." He got down in the bed, looked across at Mark a few more moments, then turned over to face the wall. "Sorry if I woke you."

It was quiet. "Is something going on around here?" Mark said finally.

"Where."

"Lisa comes up, you come up; I just wondered if something was going on I should know about."

"No. I'm just having my vacation."

After a few moments the light went out again; then there was a squeak of springs as Mark got down under his covers again.

William turned over on his back. He looked up toward the ceiling, listening to Mark's breathing in the other bed.

A day last spring. May? early June? Sitting at my desk. The quotation board broken. Some event, a death, assassination? Whose. A boring morning. Harvey Linder at the next desk, worried about something, his wife's back, a slipped disc in her back, talking all morning about it, all of us waiting for the board to be fixed, something wrong with the wiring. Everyone smoking, a depressing day, the market down unexpectedly. Something else: the death of Lewis Nell, broker two rows back, died during the night of a heart attack. Sitting there the day before, his gold phone in front of him (twenty-five years with the brokerage house to get one) talking to customers over it, friendly, fat, then the next morning Lu Anne carrying around the first morning memo, "You know, Mr. Nell had a stroke last night" (putting the memo on the desk), going on to the next desk, "Mr. Nell died last night, you know" (memo on next desk). I hardly knew him, but it made everyone depressed. The gold phone there on his desk, a mounted golf ball beside it, his pencils (shoulder rest on the receiver of the phone, a little bit of grease from his hair on the top part of the shoulder rest), all there on his desk waiting for him—depressing. Finally getting up from my desk (the electrician got the quotation board fixed sometime after twelve, after the market was closed anyway), deciding to leave for the day although not knowing where, thinking on the way down the sidewalk of going to a movie, walking to the car in the parking lot, getting in and driving back to the ivy-banked freeway (about one o'clock, not used to the way the light was that early, shadows of the other cars not the same angle as later in the afternoon), driving out the end of the freeway past gas stations, deciding not to go to a movie but to go look at neckties instead.

A fountain on the lower level of the department store, Lisa sitting on a bench against the wall looking down into the water at pennies, no one sitting beside her, an old couple down on the next seat. Seeing her, stopping (a package in her hand—it was a tablecloth, it was on the dinner table that night), standing beside a leather-covered chair, price tag Scotch-taped to its arm, suddenly seeing Lisa there, the brown sack on her lap, staring at the coins, not moving, seeing her in a different way: like the shadows at a different angle on the freeway being a different time. Lisa also being different than ever before—an unexpected time and place to see her, a young tired wife sitting, staring at a wishing pool—in the center a white clay urn rising up from the coins and the plastic ferns growing out of it and Lisa not happy, not making dinner, not talking on the phone, not having a shower or making a dress, but sitting and staring at one thirty on a Tuesday afternoon, probably on a day for her no different than the other days of the week. Stepping back around to the other side of a leather-covered couch and looking at her, customers passing between us, not wanting to go up to her or see her, watching her stare at water, then turning away, walking around through the furniture department and to the elevators, going up, getting off, the cosmetics department, girls behind counters, not staring but smiling, not looking tired like Lisa, walking on past them to the men's department and to tie racks, staring at ties (May I help you—no), finding one, "a quiet stripe" ha! (stone dead, but the gold phone ringing anyway—what is a client to think, "Your stock has gone up three points but your broker is dead" or "Your stock has gone down three points but your broker died"; Dear God don't let any of his stocks go down so his customers won't be mad at him in death). A quiet stripe—five dollars, thank you, cash or charge, thank you, thank you, yes I'll take it, no that will be all, no I don't need any handkerchiefs. Then back between two aisles of cosmetics in glass cases, girls, smiling, evenly spaced, standing behind the jars, tubes, bottles, aerosol cans, compacts, sprays—Sir? Yes? Something for your wife? (sitting underneath us, under this floor, staring through water). What do you have, here's a nice item, oh yes, it's a cream but it's a new cream, oh? yes it's brand-new cream, you may have seen the full-page ad in (Mr. Nell? I'm sorry . . . Who is calling please. Yes, well let me transfer you to one of the other brokers).

Just dab a little on your hand oh yes smell? Oh yes rub in yes introductory offer nice breasts on this one, larger than Lisa's you see it moistens in a new way, not in the old way, of course being a man you wouldn't ha ha ha. I stand, depressed, my new tie in its sack, Lisa sitting underneath staring at the fountain in this public place, me staring at this girl's breasts through her sky-blue sweater yes I'll take some thank you very much (she likes me) something else? no just that cash or charge.

Was she still there? Did I even go back. Yes, the cream. Here's some cream from upstairs guaranteed to moisten you. Hurrying down the stairs this time, past a print of a gondola, the cream (the magic cream) in one hand, tie in the other ("Lisa, hi. I saw you there. Apparently they have a special on some new kind of cream upstairs so I . . ."). Gone. Imprint of her buttocks in the green velvet cushion. Lowering the cream, the magic cream, in its sack, to my side.

What were those days like? (those days last spring). Were they like these days? Five months ago. Were those special days? Why am I thinking about those days. The gold phone ringing (I haven't thought of that since the day it happened—why now). What day of the week was it? How do I know it was Tuesday.

The movie:

Parking first, at a paint store across the street from the theatre, worrying that they would know I wasn't buying paint and tow my car away. Leaving the tie in its sack and the jar of cream in its sack in the car, locking the doors. Going in the paint store first (these aren't the kind of people who would tow your car away—are they?). I HAVE TO SEE THAT MOVIE (disturbed that day, more than usual—tits bursting against light blue wool, bursting, but not for me). Walking along in front of the theatre, glancing at the posters of women, kneeling, facing forward, smiling with bright red lips painted on black-and-white bodies, the only other color two green spots at the end of each breast to prevent you from seeing if you don't go inside (what the hell am I doing here), then walking to the end of the block, looking at my wristwatch (cars passing, whose cars, do I know that person, or do I know the back of that person's head?). Look at your watch, turn and walk back: the poster on the other side, the large black-and-white middle-aged woman beckoning me with motionless finger to enter. Glance up at the ticket booth—four dollars, an old woman in there, reading (what will she think of me—I wish I had a toothpick in my mouth). Who's inside: bums, perverts, the City Fathers? I have to go in—wait till there's a red light at both corners so no cars are passing as I go up to the booth (turn my collar up). This is ridiculous. I'll get the money out first; walking to the corner, the doorway of a bus station, looking up and down (why?), getting out the wallet and four dollar bills, returning the wallet. Is Lisa doing more shopping? In some other part of Pasadena is she pricing window shades? No cars this way, no cars the other except an old one, too old for anyone I know. Back past the bus station, right turn and now walking up over the upward-slanting rubber flooring material and up to the woman, who lowers her LOOK *magazine (one please), four bills under the glass, waiting, where's my ticket? She points down beside the booth, a turnstile: "Oh; right." Wondering why they don't have tickets I push through the turnstile, feeling the hard length of steel against my thigh (I'm inside). Clank.*

Music.

What if I see someone inside I know. What if I'm attacked. Which would be worse.

The door of a men's room, painted shiny brown—God only knows what goes on in there. More posters on the wall, more black-and-white ladies, but this time smiling down at me without dabs of paint on their nipples (I'm in).

Dead ahead a glass counter—I walk toward it—an old man standing behind, gray-haired, unhealthy look-

ing. In front of him, lined up side by side on the top of the counter, five cartons of popcorn (this is incredible) and underneath the glass top of the counter a small assortment of neatly arranged Hersheys and ju-ju-bee boxes (here, popcorn and candy, here too, *my God). "No thank you."*

Not wanting to go inside just yet, something about standing in the lobby, the two of us, the old man and I, separated by five cartons of gray cold popcorn, "Grand Canyon Suite" coming out of a loudspeaker up over his head, scratchy, something about this moment to preserve, the gray nude ladies all around us and cars passing outside in the street but us, we two, alone, not speaking, youth, age. Clank, the turnstile. I glance back: some guy in a jacket has just come through, bends down over a water fountain just inside the turnstile, some letters on the back of his jacket in dingy white felt spell out YOKOHAMA (why am I making a big thing of this —driving by I've read the marquee THE OAKS THEATRE NUDES THE WAY YOU LIKE THEM ALL NEW SHOW EVERY FRI since we've lived here —I've thought of coming here some day and seeing what it was like and now I have come and I'm inside and it's like this (but why today). Finished his water, he walks wiping his mouth past me and in through a curtain on the left.

A new song: what is it. I know the words: "You're the . . ." No. "If only . . ." No. "Mr. Wonderful, that's you." Yes. A turn right and walk to the curtain. I push it aside, gradually so as not to disturb any of the patrons inside with a sudden annoying beam of light.

I step in.

The screen. I'm looking at the screen and in color her head and her chest and with her two hands she's squeezing her breasts and running her tongue back and forth over her lips, where shall I sit. "Mr. Wonderful, that's you." It's me, I'm Mr. Wonderful. In the center? At the side? Where am I least likely to be attacked. The camera's moving down along her body. The navel, and farther; my God I've got to find a seat. Down to the center and take an aisle seat, no one directly behind me, somebody two rows down but no one within arm's length. I look up and just as the camera moves down and a dark area (it is very close, the screen is all white, all flesh, from a few inches out) but just as giant hairs start at the bottom of the screen there is a clicking, then white numbers dancing around on a black screen, then nothing.

"Boooooo."

It starts up, though, almost immediately, this time the girl is a redhead and she walks in a raincoat toward a couch. She turns, smiles, tosses her head. Slowly she unbuttons the coat and lets it fall down over her body, leaving her in black underpants and a black bra ("Mr. Wonderful, that's . . ." what are the rest of the words; if I could remember them I would enjoy this more). Off comes the bra, she doesn't waste time. A few teasing tugs at the elastic of the panties and then quickly off, tossed to the side. Down on the couch on her back. New camera angle: we are four or five inches from her crotch, which fills the screen, her fingers moving up and down over her thighs. This is more like it. The new song is "Tea for Two," an old and quavering recording. She keeps rubbing—same camera angle, you can see a little way up into her, although not far, modesty prevents her from showing us all the way up, also lighting problems, but there it is, a red pubis. An undulating movement starts (fantastic). Who would take pictures like this? What would you say to the girl? A man walks down the aisle past me with one of the boxes of popcorn from the lobby. He sits, starts eating it, looking up at the undulating groin.

(What am I doing in this place—Lisa isn't shopping somewhere, she's home crying; I know her that well anyway).

Two exit doors, one at each side of the screen, an old man walking down the aisle on the other side and pushing his way out into the alley past a gigantic brown nipple, a bell rings in the lobby as the exit door is opened ("Mr. Nell? He's dead. Will you speak with anyone else?") The bell continues ringing as the door scrapes back shut, then clank and the bell in the lobby is quiet — signifying to the old man that no one is sneaking into his palace from the rear. Do women ever come in here? I didn't notice a ladies' room. A new song: "O-o-o-o-o-klahoma, where the wind comes right behind the rain" (just the music, no lyrics, but the lyrics are there in the notes). A new girl too; short blond hair, wearing a chemise (if that's the word), sashaying forward toward the camera fiddling with the ribbon at her breasts, unties it, opens the garment to show one breast, then the other (one looks not unlike the other), she glances coquettishly down at one of them, lets the chemise fall down and out of sight toward the floor — is someone masturbating behind me? "We know we belong to the land, and the land we belong to is grand!" Who's sitting behind me—it looked like another person in a business suit as I came down the aisle although my eyes weren't well enough adjusted to be sure (glad to be not the only person wearing a suit); businessmen don't masturbate, I think it's someone over by the wall, if I could turn my head inconspicuously —I settle down farther in the chair, I turn my head: over by the wall, an old man in a jacket leaning forward and looking down into his lap, the colors from the screen dancing against the top of his gray hair as he jiggles. I watch him for several moments, then slowly turn my head back toward the screen where the girl is bent forward, her hand on the edge of a sink (how did she get in the kitchen), as the camera holds steady for a rear shot, back and forth she sways as the camera, from below, moves slowly in toward her organs (he's still masturbating, you can hear him, a clicking sound from his seat gives him away, maybe he doesn't even care, maybe you're supposed to—now someone else is doing it down in the front, his leg hooked over the seat in front of him, you can tell by the way he's sit-

ting that he's masturbating, or am I going crazy). I shouldn't be in this place, the girl now looking down between her legs, smiling, breasts, their undersides seen from below, swaying back and forth, she smiles, a frozen smile, her organ partially open (why am I watching this). There's no music, what happened to the music, just her, a whirring projector, a clicking seat where an old man works toward an orgasm, smoke in the air. Again the music, thank God. What song is that. Violins. ". . . spend the . . ." What is it: ". . . dreaming of a . . ." ". . . reverie . . ." I should go home now. This place is too sick. I need to go to the bathroom but not in there, not in through the shiny brown door, if they masturbate in here what are they doing in there. ". . . spend the lonely hours . . ." She's just standing there, the camera pointing up from under her legs, swaying back and forth, red lips smiling down, the camera angle making me nauseous (no one should take pictures like this). I won't let myself go to the bathroom till I figure out the name of this song. ". . . and each kiss an inspiration . . ." What's happening to me. A nervous feeling, an anxious feeling, is someone going to come over to me? Are people looking at me? They saw me looking at the old man masturbate—what business do you have watching him, fella—four dollars to be in a sick state of mind, how could I have come in this place. I'm helpless. Someone's going to stab me: the man a few rows back in the business suit, right now he's getting a pocket knife out of his inside suit pocket, lowering it into his lap, very carefully opening it, keeping his hands over the blade as he opens it to muffle any sound and keep the edge from flashing in the light, now moving it slowly back up along his chest, sucking in his breath with the excitement of it, deciding which place in my back to plunge it, now suddenly rising up from his chair, lunging down the aisle knife held high above his head, slavering, his eyes glittering, then yelling as with all his strength he slashes the razor-sharp knife down through the air toward my neck and then deep—"Deep Purple" of course. I thought of it; I can go to the bathroom now. I get up, the chair seat squeaks and slaps back up into place. "Sometimes I wonder why I spend the lonely hours dreaming of a song." Up past the others (the first time I get to see their faces), some of them glancing at me as I walk past, mostly older men, mostly bums, a few businessmen here and there, a burly guy slouched back in his seat with his legs sticking out into the aisle—I walk around them, up to the curtain past a blond guy with long hair and a white T-shirt listening to "Deep Purple" and looking up at the girl's crotch (I can tell it's still the same shot because of the light against his T-shirt) and into the lobby and toward the men's room door, passing the glass counter where someone is making up his mind between a Hershey and a box of ju ju bees, to the men's room. I hear water running inside—I don't want to go in if there's someone else in there but I don't want to seem chicken to the man at the counter — pushing open the door, a man in Levi's washing his hands, he looks honest, like a furnace repairman between jobs, but under the toilet stall are two legs; I walk to the urinal keeping my eyes on the tile floor (my back to the furnace repairman but I am at the peak of alertness, if he makes for me I am ready, I will listen and at the slightest sound of him coming for me I will whirl, hit him in the face with my elbow and run). I unzip my fly and wait, I'm too tensed up to go, come on, come on, listen to the sound of the water, that's it, there, stay alert but try and relax below the waist — he finishes washing his hands and pulls paper out and dries them and then walks out. Now the one in the stall is coming out (I didn't hear him wipe himself — something's funny here), out he comes and up to a mirror beside the urinal, without turning my head I can tell two things about him, that he's middle-aged and wearing a bright blue sweater, turtleneck. He starts combing his hair, a shoulder-high partition separating us — I glance over — oh God he was waiting for me to look at him, looking straight back he smiles as our eyes meet, why the hell did I look at him —

finish up here prematurely, back in the pants, zipper up the fly. Turn around—I know he's looking at me. I want to wash my hands but I have to weigh the alternatives—any delay and he'll move in, I'm sure of it, anything that could be interpreted as faltering and he'll be on me. Straight to the door with unwashed hands and pull it open, don't look back, let it close behind. In the lobby again. Safe (there were no obscenities written on the walls in there). Now home? A candy bar (I walk up to the old man at the counter). Hershey. Fifteen cents. These are wrapped at the factory, they can't be contaminated. Wrapped in a white paper, then enclosed in a brown sleeve, all at the factory, but how long has it been sitting in the lobby—how long does it take a germ to go inside a brown sleeve and in a piece of wax paper. I should get my seat before the queer comes out. Back in through the curtain. The old man against the wall, finished masturbating now, sitting back, enjoying the show (ecstasy). I'll sit closer to the front this time. Someone at the far end of this row. If the queer comes after me from the other side he'll have to pass the person in the far seat: this will slow him down. I sit, then glance behind. The curtain opens, the man in the blue turtleneck walks in. Keeping my head turned and just at a low-enough angle so he won't notice, I watch him walk down the aisle. He turns into a row of seats, walks toward the center and sits beside someone. He says something to the other person. A friend, another queer. I'm safe, free. I turn around, look up at the screen, open the Hershey bar, drop the brown sleeve and wax paper on the seat beside me, stretch my legs out into the aisle, take a first bite of the Hershey (it's fresh!) chew it, almonds. A new girl on the screen, a new song, an empty bladder. A beautiful girl, the most beautiful blackhaired girl I've ever seen, on a couch, beckoning me. What breasts! So innocent! Young—probably fresh out of college. Camera moves down to her groin. A new bite of milk chocolate. She starts to gyrate. Maybe she didn't go to college. ("They asked me how I knew, that your love was true. . . .") I should have started coming here long ago—I'll start now. Every day in this front seat eating chocolate and listening to the music, naked bodies moving above my chair. And the other people here: beautiful—minding their own business, masturbating if they feel like it, uninhibited, a brotherhood of old, young, white, brown, black, yellow (the man at the other end of my row is Chinese), all over eighteen, joined together, watching another girl come naked and huge onto the screen; down on her back, throwing open her legs. Pumping. God what a beautiful organ.

Driving home in thick traffic: how can I get Lisa into bed before dinner without being obvious. It's unbearable, the pain, I could masturbate at the next stop light, or as I'm driving. I'll walk in the apartment, grab her, throw her onto the bed. "Don't ask questions, just open your legs, if you've ever done anything for me, do this, I'll explain later." They shouldn't show those movies —someone should call the cops and tell them what they're showing, the police couldn't know, the mayor should be told, someone, it's not healthy, the citizens driving around in their cars trying to keep from masturbating in rush-hour traffic. I'm not concentrating on my driving, nearly hit that old lady's bumper. Just home to Lisa. "Come to bed, I love you . . . quickly." If I could do it with her a few times and get my mind back on important things. I'd like to do strange positions, I'm really charged up, how could I tell her I wanted to do strange positions: there's no subtle way to tell her. Rape her? Give her the cream, rub it all over her, rip off her clothes, tear them, standing up shove it into her beside the stove. Squirming, dripping (that last girl, the kind of breasts you don't believe really exist—so mammoth, rubbing them back and forth on the rug, rolling over and over toward the camera). Work tomorrow, up early —I've had a lapse today. Four dollars. A crummy feeling. Queers. This is no good. No more; that's it on the dirty movies. As of now: I hereby decide never again to go into that place, never again to waste four dollars and an afternoon. I wanted to see it, I did see it. I was titillated (that last pair of breasts—worth all four dollars — teacup nipples) but I'm not the kind of person who goes to those movies. I'm a broker. I'm married. I'm intelligent. I have will power. I've seen the inside of vaginas now, that's it, no more.

"It's some kind of cream. I got the tie and was going back out and they said it was some kind of cream for your wife. You don't have to use it, Lisa, you don't have to use it. It was a sale, introducing a new kind of cream. If you don't like the smell I said you don't have to use it. Yes, I'm ready for dinner; let me wash my hands.

"Lisa, I told you because I don't think there's any reason to have secrets from each other. I wasn't boasting. I know it was a waste of money. No, I didn't enjoy it, I'm sorry I went. I just thought you had a sense of humor. If you don't think it's funny to have a theatre full of derelicts listening to the 'Grand Canyon Suite' and watching nude women then I'm sorry I brought it up. No, I don't think it has anything to do with us that I went. How could it. I didn't stop and see you at the store because I was in a hurry to get the tie. When I came back down you were gone. Lisa? I'm sorry I even . . . next time I'll say I was at the brokerage all day. I'll lie to you, Lisa, if that's what you want. If all we can do is lie to each other to keep from upsetting the other one then let's do it that way. Don't cry, Lisa. Yes, I like the tablecloth, I said I liked it. But how much can a person like a tablecloth (picking up the corner of it, standing). How much, Lisa. Well don't you think I'm going through a little anguish too since the marriage? No, I don't know why. Do you think I like going into a movie like that? Do you think I like myself for it? Feel proud of myself sitting among old men masturbating, Lisa? Don't cry. I'm not accusing you of anything*—why do you keep saying that. There's nothing wrong with your body, or sex with you. Lisa,*

forget I brought it up. Why are you leaving the table. Lisa, I know you're unhappy, I don't know why or I'd try and help you. I don't think you're on the verge of a nervous breakdown. You're tired, I'm tired, that's all. Do you want me to apologize for going to the movie? I apologize. Yes, I mean it. But why should I apologize. Why should I apologize to you for what I do. I didn't even have to tell *you what I did. Where are you going, Lisa?"*

Then sitting, eating slowly the cold dinner off the plate on the new tablecloth; sitting in the chair at the table afterwards. Just sitting with the dirty plate in front of me, an occasional thought of a swaying breast, a dark groin, a face, a smile. Then getting up, finally, after an hour, more than an hour, walking down the hallway to the bathroom, the closed door, knocking. "Lisa?" No answer. "I just had an idea, Lisa." Still no answer. Wanting to shout at her, scream at her, break in and kill her, but instead saying, softly, "Lisa, I think we should talk about taking a short vacation."

FIVE

Next morning Nan invited William to come along with them to play tennis (the Morrises were in the habit of a tennis game every Saturday morning). After breakfast Chester went to his closet for an extra pair of tennis shoes, shorts and a T-shirt. He put them in a bag with his own equipment; then they left.

The tennis club where Nan and Chester had a membership was the Valley Hunt Club in Pasadena, and although William had driven past it many times he had never been inside. When they arrived Chester drove into a parking lot. He and Nan walked in first, with William and Lisa following, so they could show them the front hallway of the club and a large ballroom, with mirrors running along the walls, where, Nan explained as they walked through, a coming-out party for young debutantes was held each Christmas season. They looked into a bar with paneled wooden walls, then stepped out beside the club's swimming pool.

The dressing rooms were behind the courts. Lisa and Nan turned off into the women's room, then Chester gestured ahead of them with his tennis racket and he and William walked into the men's changing room. Inside Chester led the way past several rows of lockers and stopped at one in the corner. He opened it with a key and lifted out a tennis racket to hand to William. "It's an old one," he said, putting his foot up on a metal bench to untie his shoe, "but the strings were tightened last fall." He took off both leather shoes, then took off his shirt and pants. He unzipped his bag and pulled out a jock strap, letting his shorts fall to the floor and quickly pulling the strap on. "Let me get your gear out," he said, reaching into the bag again and pulling out the white shirt and shorts and tennis shoes that were for William.

"I can wear my own pants," William said.

Chester held out the white shorts. "I think you'll have more freedom in these."

William seated himself on the bench and bent over to untie one of his shoes.

"Do what you want." Chester set down the clothes, then reached into the locker for another pair of white shorts. He pulled them on, then pushed his arms and head through the holes of a T-shirt and pulled it down over his chest. "We're getting a hell of a lot of use out of this club," he said, seating himself and working a sneaker onto one of his feet. "At first I thought it would be a bust, but we use it every weekend." He wiggled on the other shoe, then bent over to tie them. "They have an out-of-this-world buffet supper here on Wednesday evenings. We'll have to bring you and Lisa over for that." He finished tying his sneakers. "I may head on out to the courts," he said.

"Go ahead."

Hitting the strings of his racket against the palm of

his hand, Chester started toward the door. "Oops." He turned around, came back to the locker and reached in for a white visored cap. He put it on, looked into a mirror hanging on the end of the lockers to adjust it, then left the room.

William changed neither his pants, which were olive colored, nor his shirt, which was a blue and white striped sport shirt. When he had gotten Chester's extra pair of sneakers on and had tied them he sat a few moments longer on the bench, looking down at the racket beside him, then picked it up and walked slowly across the black rubber mats to the door.

Lisa was wearing a pleated white tennis dress of her sister's and Nan was dressed in a straight white tennis dress, and the three of them, the two girls on one side of the net and Chester on the other, were having a rally when William came out. He walked along the fence in back of the courts, then opened a wire gate and stepped through it. Nan was running for a ball that her husband had just hit over the net. She hit it back, then turned to William. "Is boys against the girls all right with you?" She suddenly stopped and lowered her racket. "Where are the other clothes."

William closed the gate.

"Didn't they fit?"

Lisa picked up a ball, bounced it, then hit it across the net to her brother-in-law.

"Boys against the girls is fine," William said. He started along beside a white line toward the opposite court, where Chester was standing.

"Bill?" Nan said.

He stopped.

She walked up toward him. "Didn't the other clothes fit?"

William looked down at a button on his shirt. "I don't know if they did or not."

"Darling," Nan called over the net to Chester, "he can't wear these."

Chester hit back a ball to Lisa. She returned it and

Chester backed up, swung and hit it into the net. "Good shot," he said.

"Chester, he cannot wear these clothes on the court."

"What?"

"Will you come here please?"

Chester walked toward the metal post at the side where Nan and William were standing.

"Why doesn't Bill have on the white clothes that we brought for him."

Chester looked at William's pants. "He said he wanted to wear his own."

"Well we can't play till he has on the white clothes." She stood facing her husband.

Finally Chester turned and looked at some empty chairs on the other side of the fence. "No one's . . ."

"I'm sorry, Chester; tell him to go put on the right clothes."

William removed a small paper cup from a cupholder beside him, held it under the spigot on a water dispenser till it was full, then raised it to his lips and drank.

"Bill," Nan said, smiling at him, "I'm sorry, but you don't come as a guest to our club and wear dark clothes on the court; I guess you didn't know that; we'll wait for you to change before we begin."

William dropped the empty cup in a small receptacle, then looked back at her.

"Lisa?" Nan said, turning quickly away from him. "Could I speak to you?"

Lisa served a ball against the fence, then walked toward them.

"Over here," her sister said. She took her over to the other side of the net and began talking to her in a low voice.

"Actually," Chester said, "we're still just junior members. If we were full members it probably wouldn't bother her so much." He bounced his racket on the court, then caught it. "It's kind of silly, but we really have to be careful about making the right impression at first—that's Nan's feeling, I more or less think it would be good if we went along with it."

"The right impression on the other members."

"That's it," he said. "So if it wouldn't make that much difference to you . . ."

William spun his racket, let it fall to the court, then picked it up. "How do you get to be full members."

"They vote," Chester said. "The committee votes."

"How do you get to be junior members."

"We applied. We had a sponsor. The committee voted when our names came up."

"Who was your sponsor." William tossed his racket up and caught it.

"Someone named Tanner," Chester said. "Actually, he's an ex-president of the club."

"Why isn't he any more."

"President?"

"Yes."

"Oh. Well he rotated."

"And when do you go from being a junior to a full member."

"After six months we can apply," he said. "So if it's just the same to you to put on the light-colored clothes . . ."

Lisa walked up beside them. "Could I speak to you?"

"Chester?" Nan called. "Shall we rally please?"

Chester hurried back to the court where he had been before, just in time to return a fast ball from his wife.

William followed Lisa over to where two white lines converged at the end of the court. "Why didn't you wear the white clothes."

"I didn't want to."

"Why."

"I wanted to stay in these."

Lisa glanced at her sister, then back at William. "Will you change?"

"What for."

"Because we're guests."

William rested the end of his racket on the court.

"Will you change?" she said. "They're waiting."

He stood looking down at her. The ball bounced several times back and forth between Nan and Chester. "I feel comfortable in these."

Lisa glanced at Nan as she hurried past them for a ball. "Have you chosen this particular time and place to make some kind of stand? If you have, it's the wrong time, the worst place, and the most inconsiderate way you could do it."

"What are we here playing tennis for," William said.

"We were invited."

"We don't like tennis," he said. "I don't like it, you don't like it."

"You should have thought of that before." She turned and started back toward her sister.

"Lisa?"

She stopped.

"Come back." He motioned for her to return and she walked back. "You don't like tennis, do you."

"I don't mind it."

"You hate it," he said. "We've played twice; you've said after each time you hate it."

"It won't kill me to play."

"Why do we do things we don't like to do."

She looked back at Chester, who was getting a drink from the drinking fountain.

"Why," he said, "when we basically don't want to do them."

"Because there's such a thing as courtesy," she said.

William tucked the racket under his arm. "We're at a place we don't want to be playing a game we don't want to play. Why, Lisa."

"They wanted us to see their club."

"We've seen clubs before. What are we doing here, Lisa."

"Will you change your clothes or not."

"If you tell me why we are here."

"We were invited here; we didn't want to hurt their feelings."

He shook his head. "That's not good enough. The dark clothes stay on." He looked across the court beside them to a far one beyond it. "I'll play down there." he said. "Tell them I'll compromise and play down there."

Lisa looked down at the far court. "Why down there."

"It's shady down there," he said. "The other members won't notice the color of my clothes as well down there."

Lisa looked at William a moment, then walked back toward Nan.

"Everything straightened out?"

"He says he'll play down on that other court."

Nan turned to look at the far court. "It makes no difference which court we use; does he understand he's not to wear those clothes?"

"No."

William pointed down at the shaded court at the far end. "That one."

"Shall we get started?" Chester said.

"Let's go down to the far court," William said, "and get started."

Chester glanced down at it. "Okay," he said. He picked up a ball.

"Is that all right, Nan?" William said.

Lisa and Chester went ahead toward the shaded court.

"Is that all right?" William said again.

Nan looked for a moment at her husband and Lisa walking away, then quickly at William, then started after the others.

"Does that solve the problem of the dark clothes," William said, walking beside her, "keeping in the shade so the other members won't notice."

"Shall Lisa and I serve?" Nan called to her husband as they reached the court.

"I'll spin." Chester stopped and spun his racket. "Call it!"

"Rough," Nan said.

He bent over and looked at the racket's strings when it had fallen to the asphalt. "Rough it is."

"We serve," Nan said to her sister.

"Go ahead."

Nan held up her hand. "Balls please?"

"I just wanted to be sure it's all right now about the clothes," William said. "Some verbal acknowledgment, Nan, is what I'm waiting for—just a gesture of courtesy on your part."

A ball bounced toward Nan from her husband and she caught it. A second one came and she caught the second one. "Thank you." She carried them to the line at the end of the court and stood, bouncing them, while Lisa walked up to the net.

"Shall I play right side?" Chester said.

"Whichever you'd like." William walked to the rear of the court, into the shade, and turned around to face the net.

"May I take two?" Nan called.

"Go ahead."

She tossed up a ball and hit it across the net. Chester caught it and waited for a second one. When the second one came he caught it and tossed them back. "This will go," Nan said when she had both balls back. She tossed up the ball and hit it in the direction of Chester.

"Long!" he said.

She stepped back to the line again, threw up her second ball and hit it, more lightly then before. It fell into the court. Chester ran forward and hit it to Lisa. Lisa jumped sideways, holding out her racket, and the ball bounced back into Chester's court. Chester hit it to his wife. She backed up several feet and swung, hitting it very hard across the net and toward William. It struck near the center of the court, then bounced on past William's elbow, as he stood, the end of his racket resting on the point of his shoe. "He didn't try to hit it," Nan said.

William cleared his throat. "I still didn't hear you answer my question," he said. "Is it all right about the dark clothes now."

The other three stood where they were, looking at him. It was quiet for a few moments, then Chester turned around and picked up the ball. "Fifteen, love." He batted it across the net to his wife, but she let it go by.

"Chester? Could I speak to you a moment?"

"Fifteen, love," he said. "Come on, let's play tennis." Chester walked back to his line and crouched over slightly, holding the racket in front of him.

Finally Nan picked up the ball, returned to the service line and served it into William's court. It bounced past his left shoulder. "There are several things I've wanted to discuss since coming up here yesterday," William said. "It's been difficult to bring them up, but I think this is the right time."

"Thirty, love." Chester retrieved the ball and threw it across the net. "Here we go; thirty, love."

"The first thing," William said, "is that I'm grateful for your hospitality, not just yesterday and today, but since Lisa and I have been married. Because of the atmosphere, it's hard to show gratitude, but I realize we both owe you a lot."

Nan picked up a ball. "This is very touching," she said, "and we'll hear it after we're finished playing. Service?" She stepped back to the line, tossed up the ball and served it toward her husband.

"No, dear," he said as it bounced.

She hit another. Chester sent it back and she returned it. Again it passed between them and then Chester hit it to Lisa, who was at the net. She held up her racket. The ball bounced off it and toward William, hitting his knee, then falling dead on the court.

"Whatever else I may say," he said, "I owe a lot to both of you for being around as Lisa and I were getting started in our marriage."

"What's that now," Chester said, "forty, love?" He walked up for the ball.

"However," William said, "along with your kindnesses to us . . ."

Chester tossed the ball back to his wife.

"I'll serve again to you," she said.

"Along with these," William said, "I would have to say there's been a certain feeling which hasn't ever quite been defined, but I think perhaps it would be healthy if it was now."

"Service!" Nan hit the ball into the net.

"I don't know what this feeling is exactly," William said, "but I think it's what Lisa was trying to say to us last night at dinner."

"Service again!" Nan tossed up another ball and hit it.

"Wide!" her husband said.

"Score?" Nan held out her hand for the ball.

"Forty, five." He hit it back to her.

"There's a certain quality to the way we all act with each other that's causing trouble. If it weren't causing problems between myself and Lisa I wouldn't worry about it. It is, though, and I don't intend to have it go on."

"Service!" Nan served a hard ball into the court. Her husband swung at it but hit it off over her head and against the fence.

"Good, dear; very good serve." He ran forward to get a new ball for her.

"I don't object to your way of life," William said.

"Is that game?" Nan said.

Chester held up his hand. "I'll serve."

"I don't object to your house, your tennis club, your car, your yard, your street, your clothes, or your furniture." He held up his racket. "But there is something that I object to."

"Taking two," Chester said, serving a ball into the fence.

"I object to being told how to arrange my life and my thinking, and it was some things Lisa said last night at dinner that helped me more than anything else to see this, because I've done it to others, just as they've done it to me; maybe it's because I was doing it to them that prevented me from seeing they were doing it to me."

"These will go," Chester said, waiting for the balls to be returned to him.

"Except for Lisa, there hasn't been one person I've ever known who hasn't told me, in one way or another, how I should think, and how I should live, and how I should somehow be more like them than like myself. I appreciate that you're not conscious of what you're doing, but I'm not going to take it any more."

"Serving," Chester said.

Lisa was still at the net, watching her husband.

"Lisa?" Nan said. "Will you come back so he can serve to you?"

She turned and started back.

"You're insecure people," William said, "and that may be the reason you try and foist off your attitudes on anyone who comes near."

Lisa ran forward to return Chester's serve. The ball bounced in front of William as he stood there.

"Love, five," Chester said.

"I'm insecure myself, I realize that."

"Dear?" Nan said. "I really don't think this can go on."

"So," William said, "one way or another, I'm going to pry you loose." He turned and pointed at Chester. "But I'm not going to quit my job and blame the system. That would make it too easy for you."

Nan hurried up to the net. "The Tanners are coming on the next court," she said.

"I'm in this to stay, no matter how horrible you make it look, because I'll find the good in it."

"Chester," Nan said in a hoarse whisper to her husband, "he really has to get off the court."

Chester walked up to William and rested his hand on his shoulder. "Old boy . . ."

William turned to him. "I'll sit this set out."

"Thank you."

He walked toward a chair at the side of the court as Nan turned, smiling, to wave at the Tanners.

The girls beat Chester. "We were lucky," Nan said, wiping her forehead with the back of her hand.

Chester picked up a ball at the net. "A well-played set." William handed him the empty ball can from beside his chair; Chester put the ball in it and walked toward the wall to pick up another.

"Shall we shower and go?" Nan said. She walked back toward the gate at the end of the court.

William got up from the chair. He watched Chester go to the other side of the court for the final ball, then followed Nan and Lisa through the gate and along the walkway toward the dressing rooms. They turned into the room marked "Women." William waited while Chester caught up, then walked beside him toward the men's dressing room. Chester moved his arm slowly out beside him a circle. "I have a little shoulder quirk sometimes," he said. "I need to get the water on it."

They walked in through the door of the dressing room, but then William stopped.

"What a workout," Chester said.

"I'll be right back." He watched Chester pick up a towel and run it over his face, then stepped out of the dressing room again.

On the court beside the Tanners' was another foursome, two older men and ladies, all dressed in white, one of the men opening a fresh can of balls. The can made a short hissing sound. William walked back as far as the ladies' dressing room, then leaned against the wall beside the door, looking out through the wire fence.

The man took the top off the can of balls and tossed them around to the other players. William turned slightly and looked behind him through the open door of the dressing room. Inside was a white bench and a large basket with used towels in it, but there was a high partition running along beside the door and he couldn't see anything else. He looked back at the court as one of the men threw up his ball and hit it. It bounced past a woman with her back to William. She coughed as she swung at it, then the ball hit the fence several feet away from William's face. She came back to retrieve it, turned around and hit it across the net. William watched as she walked up for another ball and as a man on the far side began pulling his sweater up over his head. While it was still covering his eyes, and as the other man was bent down tying his shoe, and as the two women were facing the other way, William turned around and stepped quickly in through the door of the ladies' dressing room. Keeping his eyes to the front he moved around behind the door and pulled it back against him so he was enclosed in a small triangular space. Then he let out his breath.

He kept his hand on the handle of the door and waited nearly a minute, listening to the sound of the balls being hit back and forth on the court outside. Then he pushed the door several inches forward. He could see into a side room where there was a row of toilet stalls. Suddenly a shower was turned on. He stepped back against the wall, pulling the door toward him.

The next time he pushed it farther than before. He glanced around at the figures on the tennis court for a moment, then started slowly along beside the partition sealing off the other side of the locker room. As he neared the end of it he stopped, then moved the side of his face around to look in at several rows of steel lockers. The shower stalls were against the far wall and two of them were in use. William watched two figures on the other side of the opaque glass doors as they soaped themselves.

Then he moved his head forward and noticed a woman, dressed in an orange sweater and slacks, bent over and dusting the toe of one of her shoes. Very quickly he moved out across an open space, then into the room with the toilet stalls, bending down for a moment, long enough to see that there were no feet under any of the stall doors. He pressed himself up against the white tile wall and peered around at the woman in the orange sweater. She walked to a mirror fastened to the end of a row of lockers and patted at the back of her hair several times, then leaned up close to the glass and inspected her lips, opening and shutting her mouth as she did. As she turned away from the mirror William pressed his back against the wall and listened to her footsteps coming closer, then turning onto the wooden walk that led out the door of the dressing room. He watched as the orange sweater disappeared around the edge of the door, then after a quick look at the players out the door on the court he stepped back across the open space and to the other side of a row of beige steel lockers.

Down at the end of the lockers the two figures continued soaping themselves behind the glass doors of the shower stalls. The one in the left stall bent sideways and soaped her legs; the other one was straightened up, just standing, letting the water hit the back of her neck and then run down her body. "I think your forehand's better than last summer," Nan said, continuing to move her hands over her legs, "but you're still coming down on top of it too much." She began soaping one of her arms.

William started slowly forward.

"For every one you hit too long," Nan said, "you hit six or seven into the net. Did you notice that?"

"I hadn't."

"That's because you're coming down on it."

William reached the end of the passageway between the lockers, then stopped.

"Do you have any new ideas about Bill?" Nan said.

Lisa didn't answer.

"He needs some kind of help, that's for sure. I really thought there might have been hope for him before his performance on the tennis court, but now I seriously question that. I guess we'll just have to put up with him as best we can till he starts work again. Then we'll begin some proceedings."

Lisa continued standing under the jet of water.

"Don't you think?" Nan said.

She didn't answer.

"You can't really try to explain things to him any more," Nan said, "he's beyond that now." She began soaping her breasts. "As much as I once admired and respected him, I'm afraid I really don't have the time for him any more. I know that sounds cruel, but it's as though he no longer operates in the bounds of our kind of logic, isn't it."

William reached out slowly, took the handle of the door of his wife's stall and pulled it, just till it clicked.

"Don't you think we should just bear up as best as we can for now?" Nan said. "And discuss proceedings with Walt Hunnicutt down the street?"

William lowered his hand. Slowly the door swung open.

"I don't think it's any use to try and have Chester straighten him out. Chester has enough on his mind."

Lisa turned and began reaching for the door, then stopped and looked up at her husband.

"Chester's been a real rock through all of this."

Lisa's eyes widened.

"Lisa?" her sister said.

William held out his hand to her, then gestured for her to come toward him.

"Later today I'm going to suggest again that Bill go on back to the beach—if we all tell him I think he will."

Lisa opened her mouth to say something but William put his finger up to her lips and she was quiet. He took a step forward and reached out for her hand. He held it for a moment, then led her slowly out of the stall.

"Of course you're the one I feel sorriest for," Nan said. "I can tell you my heart sometimes breaks when I think what you're going through right now."

William spoke very softly, the sound of the driving jets of water louder than his voice. "There's a reason I came in here," he said.

Lisa glanced at the door of the other stall, then back at William.

"But I don't really feel sorry for Bill any more. After this morning he'll have to start going elsewhere for whatever sympathy he wants."

"Please go," Lisa whispered. "I'll see you later."

"Here's the reason I came in here."

Suddenly there was the sound of footsteps coming in through the door of the locker room. William grabbed his wife's arm, looked quickly around, then pulled her after him toward the corner. There was a large closet, piled high with bundles of clean towels. He pulled her inside and closed the door.

"What I think it really comes down to," Nan was saying in her shower, "is simply a sense of maturity that maybe some of us just never attain; even though we grow older in years and take on all the superficial attributes of adulthood, something inside never takes hold."

At the top of the door were four round holes in a row. William climbed up onto a bundle of towels and put his eye to the hole at one side. He watched as two women came in, one of them walking into the side room and into a toilet stall and the other coming into the locker area.

"Don't you think that's really the basis of it?" Nan said.

William watched the woman turn her head and look at Nan through the mottled glass.

"A real sense of maturity? A real sense of other people? Don't you think that's really what's at the basis of his flaw?"

The woman continued looking at the shower door for a few more moments, then walked to a locker, opened it and removed a pair of shoes. She closed the locker and carried them out, glancing at Nan through the glass as she passed her.

"I do," Nan said.

William got down from the stack of towels. Then he felt across the top of it, found a string, broke it and removed the top towel. "Dry off."

Lisa took it and began drying herself. "What happens when Nan gets out."

William placed his hands on her wet shoulders. "From now on, Lisa, we're not going to let people interfere. I promise you." From the gray light coming in through the holes at the top of the door he could see she was looking up at him.,

Nan was still talking in the shower.

"I slept with a girl yesterday," William said. "I didn't come up to apologize for it. I came up to tell you; I knew even before I did it that I'd get in the car afterwards and drive up here to tell you."

Slowly Lisa moved backwards so that her shoulders slipped out of her husband's hands. She cleared her throat.

"I was out walking," he said. "I was depressed; I don't even know who it was."

"You slept . . ." Lisa set the towel down on a pile beside her. She looked down at it a moment, then turned toward the door. "Thank you for telling me." She reached for the handle.

William took her arm.

She pulled it away. "I'm not mad," she said. "I just want to be by myself now."

He took her arm again and squeezed it. "We have to fight, Lisa. That's what we weren't doing before." He put his other hand back on her shoulder. "We were just sitting back taking it, Lisa, but now we're going to start fighting."

Suddenly she pulled away and put her hands up over her face. "Why did you do it, Bill."

"I don't know."

"Where."

"In her room."

She turned and pushed her face against the side of a stack of towels, beginning to cry. "Is it my fault?"

"No," he said, putting his arms around her, "it's their fault; that's what we have to realize. Them, Lisa. They don't want us to be happy. They want me to have affairs and they want you to divorce me. Not just those two, but all of them." He pulled her around toward him. "Believe me, Lisa." He pushed her hands away from her face and brought her mouth up against his own. "Lisa." He reached down for the buckle of his belt, undid it quickly, then pushed his pants around his hips.

"No."

"I don't care," he said, pressing up against her, "I'll do it here, I'll do it in the street, because I love you and I don't care about anything else but the two of us any more."

William opened the closet door and gestured for his wife to go out first. A woman, naked except for a pair of pink silk panties she had slid down to her ankles, looked up as Lisa stepped nude out into the locker room. "Oh," she said, "where did you come from."

William stepped out after her.

The woman threw one of her arms across her breasts. She grabbed at the panties with her other hand, trying to pull them up, but the elastic caught on one of her knees.

"It's all right," Lisa said, walking past her and to a locker, "he's my husband."

William seated himself on the end of a bench, folded his arms across his chest and smiled at the lady. "Hi," he said.

She hobbled quickly around a locker and out of sight.

Nan was at the parking lot standing beside the car. "Where have you been," she said. She walked toward them as Lisa and William appeared around the side of the building. "Chester's looking for you." They walked past her and to the car. William opened the door and held the seat forward as Lisa got in, then climbed in after her. Nan stood a moment where they had passed her. She turned around and walked to the car. "Lisa?"

Lisa smiled at her. "Where's Chester."

"Inside."

"Why don't you tell him we're here."

Nan looked in through the window at them for a few moments, then walked over to the door of the main club building and opened the door. "They're in the car," Nan said.

Chester and his wife walked back to the car and each got in. "We didn't see you after our showers," Chester said, arching up his back so he could reach into his pocket for the car keys. "I thought you might have wandered into the Hunt Room for a drink." He inserted the key into the ignition and turned it. The engine started, then he drove out of the club's parking lot and into the street.

Nan cleared her throat. She turned around in her seat, putting her elbow over the top of it, and looked at her sister. "Where," she said.

"Where what."

"Where were you when I came out of my shower."

"What's the difference," William said.

"The difference," she said, turning farther around in the seat to face him, "is that I got out of my shower, after having carried on a conversation as we were showering, to find the door open, water running out onto the floor of the locker room, and no sign of Lisa. And I want an explanation."

"Did you turn off my shower?" Lisa said.

"Yes."

"Thank you."

"Chester," Nan said, turning to her husband, "stop the car."

"What for."

"Do as I tell you." She pointed out the window. "Pull over here."

Chester put on his directional signaler, then drove over to the curb.

"Why are we stopping," William said.

"Tell me what is going on here," Nan said. "After the demonstration William put on for us out on the courts I want to know if anything else went on that I should know about."

William shook his head.

"I'm asking Lisa."

"Chester?" William said. "Lisa and I will be going back to the beach as soon as we can, so if we could get to your house I'd appreciate it."

Chester put his signaler on to indicate he was going to move back into the street.

Nan reached over and turned it off.

"We want to go back to our car now," William said.

Nan sat staring at him as traffic passed in the street. Then, finally, she turned around again to face the front. "If Bill wants to get back to the beach," she said, "I guess you'd better drive him to his car."

Chester signaled again, then turned out into the street and drove them back to San Marino. Part way back William reached out to put his arm around Lisa's shoulders, but no one spoke till they were in Nan and Chester's driveway again.

"We'd love to have you stay a little longer, Bill," Nan said, stepping out of the car onto the walk, "but if you feel you want to start back, of course that's up to you."

They all got out; then Lisa walked up to the front door, bent over to get the key from under the ceramic dog and opened the door.

"Bill?" Nan said, holding out her hand. "We're always happy to see you, and I want you to feel welcome any time at all."

William shook her hand. "That's very kind of you."

"Chester," Nan said, "Bill's leaving, why don't you see him to his car."

Chester held out his hand. "Carry on," he said, smiling.

"Same to you."

They shook hands.

"See him to his car, Chester."

Chester nodded and started down across the dichondra beside William. They reached his car, parked at the curb.

"Open the door for him, Chester."

Chester walked around to the driver's side and opened the door.

"Goodbye, Bill," Nan said, starting back up toward the house. "You won't worry a minute about Lisa, will you."

"No."

"Easy on those freeways," Chester said, gesturing for William to get in.

William climbed in under the steering wheel and Chester closed his door for him. "Take it easy now," Chester said, grinning.

"Same to you, Chester." William slid across the seat, opened the other door and stepped up onto the curb. He closed the door, then leaned against the side of his car and folded his arms across his chest.

Nan stopped. She looked at Chester a moment, then back at William. "Bill, you don't think you're taking her with you, do you; you don't think that."

"Not if she doesn't want to go with me."

"You're welcome to stay here with us, of course, but I'm not going to let anything interrupt the progress she's made in the last week. You understand that, I hope."

Lisa appeared at the front door, her suitcase in her hand.

"No," Nan said, shaking her head at her. "No, Lisa."

Lisa stepped down off the small brick porch and walked past her sister toward the car.

"Chester," Nan said, "the time's here for you to step forward and do a man's job; right now."

Chester stepped back up on the lawn. "Let's no one be hasty," he said. "There's some left-over potato salad in the icebox."

"That's not how a man does his job, Chester."

William opened the car door. Lisa set her suitcase in on the floor behind the seat, then got in.

"It's always easiest to try and run away from problems," Nan said, her voice shrill, "but you're going to find out that life's . . ."

"Goodbye," Lisa said, closing the door, looking out the open window at her sister. "I'll give you a call in a couple days."

William walked around to his side of the car. He stopped and faced toward Nan, standing with her feet planted slightly apart on the dichondra. "Do you have anything else to say to us?" he said quietly.

She looked back at him, but didn't answer.

"No?"

Her eyes stayed fixed on his across the white top of the car.

William nodded at Chester, then got in. He glanced out the window past Lisa a final time. "Goodbye, Nan," he said. Then he started the car and drove off.